# THE ALIEN WHO ATE MY HOMEWORK AND BURPED

Edited by
**Dean Wesley Smith**

# Stories from Pulphouse
### FICTION MAGAZINE

WMG
PUBLISHING

**The Alien Who Ate My Homework And Burped**

Published by WMG Publishing Inc.
All stories reprinted from the pages of
*Pulphouse Fiction Magazine*
Cover and interior design copyright © 2024 WMG Publishing, Inc.
Cover art copyright © by zahradnik | Depositphotos

ISBN 13 (Trade Paperback): 978-1-56146-994-9

# MORE FROM PULPHOUSE

## *PULPHOUSE FICTION MAGAZINE* SUBSCRIPTION

*Available in eBook and Paper subscriptions*

Go to **www.pulphousemagazine.com**

- 6 Monthly Issues in eBook
- 6 Monthly Issues in Trade Paperback
- 12 Monthly Issues in eBook
- 12 Montly Issues in Trade Paperback

## PREVIOUS PULPHOUSE ISSUES

Go to www.pulphousemagazine.com to buy any of our previous issues, including the very first Issue Zero!

## MORE STORIES FROM *PULPHOUSE FICTION MAGAZINE*

A Twist of a Knife

Alibi Murder

Aliens Among Us

Cattitude Edited

Destination Tomorrow or Yesterday

Don't Touch My Magic!

Ghosts Among Us

History Repeats for No Reason

Implode the Membrane

Jingle My Bells

No Way: Totally Twisted Tales

Run!! Creatures, Critters, and Pulphousers…

Snot-Nosed Aliens

That's Really Messed Up

There'll Be Blue Popcorn Without You!

Three Sheets to the Wind

Twisted Robots, Oh, My!

## STORIES FROM THE ORIGINAL PULPHOUSE

Stories from the Original Pulphouse: A Fiction Magazine

Stories from Pulphouse: The Hardback Magazine

# ALSO BY
## DEAN WESLEY SMITH

**COLD POKER GANG**

Kill Game

Cold Call

Calling Dead

Bad Beat

Dead Hand

Freezeout

Ace High

Burn Card

Heads Up

Ring Game

Bottom Pair

Case Card

**THE POKER BOY UNIVERSE**

POKER BOY

The Slots of Saturn: A Poker Boy Novel

They're Back: A Poker Boy Short Novel

Luck Be Ladies: A Poker Boy Collection

Playing a Hunch: A Poker Boy Collection

A Poker Boy Christmas: A Poker Boy Collection

GHOST OF A CHANCE

The Poker Chip: A Ghost of a Chance Novel

The Christmas Gift: A Ghost of a Chance Novel

The Free Meal: A Ghost of a Chance Novel

The Cop Car: A Ghost of a Chance Novella

The Deep Sunset: A Ghost of a Chance Novel

MARBLE GRANT

The First Year: A Marble Grant Novel

Time for Cool Madness: Six Crazy Marble Grant Stories

PAKHET JONES

The Big Tom: A Packet Jones Short Novel

Big Eyes: A Packet Jones Short Novel

## THUNDER MOUNTAIN

Thunder Mountain

Monumental Summit

Avalanche Creek

The Edwards Mansion

Lake Roosevelt

Warm Springs

Melody Ridge

Grapevine Springs

The Idanha Hotel

The Taft Ranch

Tombstone Canyon

Dry Creek Crossing

Hot Springs Meadow

Green Valley

**SEEDERS UNIVERSE**

Dust and Kisses: A Seeders Universe Prequel Novel

Against Time

Sector Justice

Morning Song

The High Edge

Star Mist

Star Rain

Star Fall

Starburst

Rescue Two

# CONTENTS

# INTRODUCTION

## DEAN WESLEY SMITH

Well, maybe the silliest title for an anthology I have ever come up with, and trust me, over the years I have come up with some doozies.

What is really fun about just coming up with titles and then looking through the 500 plus *Pulphouse Fiction Magazine* stories is that I always find far, far too many stories that will fit.

Far, far, far too many.

I think out of the 500 or so stories we have published so far, fifty or sixty of them would have fit perfectly.

So that's why I get the big bucks for editing (you really think I get big bucks for this, I have some land in Florida that connects a bridge in New York to sell you.)

But instead of big bucks, I get to have fun. Sorting through that many great stories, stories I loved enough to buy and put in the magazine, is like a readers best possible adventure into memory after memory after memory.

I know, without a doubt, that I am the only person on the

planet that has loved every story in *Pulphouse Fiction Magazine*. Every story because I bought them all and published them.

So deciding between one story or another is hard, granted. But at the same time great fun.

I sure hope you enjoy reading this anthology with the silly title as much as I did putting it together.

Dean Wesley Smith
Las Vegas, NV

**LIVE THE PULPHOUSE LIFE!**

Grab your Pulphouse mug and fill it with your favorite beverage and lounge in your coziest chair with the Thumper pillow while you read the latest issue of *Pulphouse*.

Want to mark off the date when your next issue will arrive? Get the *Pulphouse* calendar featuring some of our favorite *Pulphouse* cartoons!

Find all this and so much more at the *Pulphouse Fiction Magazine* online store at:

**http://pulphousemagazine.com**

*And say hi to Thumper while you're there.*

# THE ALIEN WHO
# ATE MY HOMEWORK
# AND BURPED

# FRANCESCA AND THE SENTIENT PEACHES FROM OUTER SPACE

## BONNIE ELIZABETH

In Issue #13, Bonnie Elizabeth gave us a story called "The Man Who Married His Wife's Thigh." And then she brought us sentient peaches from outer space in this story. Bonnie can really hit Pulphouse stories when she sets her mind to it.

And Pulphouse titles.

And even better, the stories are great stories. Bonnie writes in a variety of genres. Her popular Whisper series is contemporary fantasy and her Teenage Fairy Godmother series is written for teens. More information about her writing can be found at https://www.bonnieelizabeth.com

# FRANCESCA AND THE SENTIENT PEACHES FROM OUTER SPACE

BONNIE ELIZABETH

This could be Francesca's big break. She'd studied hard to be a battle chef, wielding her carving knife like a sword, her smaller, petite paring knife like a dirk. But luck had never been on Francesca's side, always getting passed over because she got sick when she ended up in weightlessness on a space ship.

It was a testament to how good Francesca was that she hadn't been cut from the program. After all, when a ship was hit, one of the first things that went was the artificial gravity.

Here in Sector Two, no one expected an encounter, leaving Francesca to do sous chef duties though she was still battle ready if there was a need. There were few Sentient Peaches left in the area. In earlier missions, heroic battle chefs had culled the fruits so that the battle gardeners could cut down the trees that had been planted across the path of the galaxy the Sentient Peaches had taken.

The scientific ship was basically a tube with a pointed end, something called cigar-shaped. In the back were two bays for the single pilot cutter ships. In the front were sleeping quarters and in the middle, the most protected area, was the bridge, engineering, and the all-important scientific bays. The kitchens were practically an afterthought, barely bigger than the one Francesca had in her student apartment. It was a disgrace.

Because of that, Francesca had hoped for a battle. Now that it was really there, and far worse than anyone expected, she hoped she'd acquit herself well and if the ship did lose gravity that her sickness wouldn't cause problems for anyone. And, of course, she hoped for a nice thick slice of Sentient Peach flesh to create her own signature dish in order to open her own chain of restaurants—although, given how far down she was in the ranks, it would probably be in Sector Nine which was mostly pirates and other sorts of criminals.

Francesca stood in the left cutter bay. The force field kept oxygen inside and the weightlessness of space outside the fan shaped room, though she could see through the field to the darkness and the stars, where they weren't blotted out by the damned Sentient Peaches. The sentient fruits were usually six to eight feet in diameter, their pink-and-orange skins all colored differently. A few of the battle-hardened chefs claimed to recognize some of the leaders. Ordinary people scoffed, but, as a battle chef herself, Francesca knew they would recognize the leaders. A single bruise here or there, a slightly green area where a stem had once been. Those were all tells to those who knew fruits.

She was surrounded by almost two dozen other battle chefs, the ship's entire complement. It was, after all, a scientific expedition ship, not a battle-kitchen ship with chefs all over the place. There were over a hundred of the Sentient Peaches out there.

4

Already four of them were clinging to the back of the ship, their golden-and-pink flesh just visible around the edges of the force field, attempting to break into the bay. The bay was large enough to hold ten of the smaller cutter ships that allowed a single chef to go out and do battle. Those had already been sent out, some of the pilot chefs flying around, using the paring knives that came out of the nose to slice and dice the Sentient Peaches.

They'd all get portions of the Sentient Peaches once the battle was done.

Francesca had on her chef's space suit, the white coverings clinging to her body, the clear face covering tickling the tip of her nose, giving her a dose of the lavender oil she'd placed in her oxygen mixer in hopes that it would calm her fears. The chef's hat helmet was ready to go if she had to squirt boiling water at the fruits when they came through.

The bay creaked and groaned around her, the peaches trying to force their way inside, pressing their pale-orange flesh against the ship's hull, letting their special acids eat away at various sections. Francesca had on gravity boots but those weren't to be turned on until gravity was gone. She had the tether that would keep her from being pulled out into space once the hull was breached in the bay.

The shiny silver metal floor was dark with the fresh oil that had been applied to the cutters, the cleaners not having a chance to go through. Their work would begin after the battle. As a scientific expedition, there were plenty of them.

Francesca felt her heart race, as she mentally traced the outline of the oil patterns, remembering the ships that had been there. Her friend Graciella was a pilot chef. The two women had worked together in culinary battle school, slicing and dicing side by side, Francesca always just far enough ahead that Graciella had no chance against her. Instead, because she could handle the lack of gravity, Graciella had taken to being a pilot chef rather than the more prestigious battle chefs.

The outline of oil around the spaces reminded Francesca of the tracings around dead bodies she saw in the vids she sometimes watched. One of her favorites was about one of the early murderous Sentient Peaches. They hated that humans wanted to eat their flesh. Before they'd gotten interstellar space flight capabilities, the peaches would sneak up on humans and suffocate them with their soft and furry flesh pressing into their mouths and noses. In this particular movie, the Sentient Peach was willing to die for its cause. Francesca knew the filmmaker was hoping to create some sympathy for the enemy, but who could feel sorry for the sweet and juicy monsters?

The rest of the bay floor was a paler silver and the walls, those not a force field, were a standard white like the halls of the ship she was on. The white got tiring on the eyes, but fortunately, at least, Francesca's quarters were too small and cramped for her to notice in there. Waiting in the bay, with the bright lights, where the shiny white walls seemed to wink at her if the light flickered, which it did because the peaches were slowly destroying the outer wall, made her head throb.

A thump reached the ship as several of the large peaches, those rose-and-gold spheres, hit the force field. Several bounced off into space. Francesca even saw one cut down by a cutter, the sleek narrow ship with the knife at the nose was hard for the round peaches to crush. It could too easily pierce their spongy flesh and skewer the seed of their sentience at their core.

6

Francesca supposed she could understand why the Peaches hated humans. She'd hate anyone who wanted to destroy and devour her family and friends, too. But the Sentient Peaches had never wanted a truce. They'd never come out and explained they'd become sentient. They'd just expected humans to know. And then they'd gotten interstellar space flight first, fleeing the solar system of old Earth to plant their seeds across the path they took as they traveled through the galaxy, leaving behind ever larger, juicier, and more flavorful fruit. It seemed as if the angrier the fruit got, the tastier its flesh.

Francesca felt her stomach rise into her throat as the gravity went out. She supposed it had been too much to hope that she wouldn't end up getting sick. She turned on her gravity boots before she'd even floated an inch, much faster than the other battle chefs. Still, she felt dizzy and the white walls were looking fuzzy.

She shook her head but the fuzzy walls didn't change. Only their color.

Something pulled Francesca forward, though she hadn't lifted one of her boots. The air was being sucked out of the bay. The Sentient Peaches had breached.

She'd barely had time to process the breach when she was pulled towards the huge spherical creatures entering the bay, their size and flesh proof against the vacuum of space, the smaller fruits clinging to the walls as they rolled themselves inside.

Francesca held her cleaver out forward, as she'd been taught. The other battle chefs waved theirs around. One got a cut of peach flesh, too small to do anything but annoy the creature. Another chopped the arm off his fellow chef.

7

Fortunately, neither of those chefs was anywhere near Francesca.

She slammed into one of the large rolling peaches. It threatened to roll over her body as it came in and the vacuum of space was attempting to pull her out, only the tether at her back keeping her from worrying about being lost in the battle forever.

Even so, she couldn't push herself backwards, so she pushed herself up, letting the creature roll under her feet as she balanced on it like an old-time logger dancing on logs in a river. The flesh was a lovely shade of pink and squishy enough that Francesca knew this fruit was getting old.

She leaped up and then let her boots drag her down again on it. Orange-and-gold flesh spattered around her, and the thing made a high-pitched squeal that reached her ears even through the noisy hum of her helmet.

Grabbing the skewer from her back, Francesca plunged it down into through the remaining peachy-gold flesh and into the harder, brown pit below. When the fruit stopped moving, she pulled her skewer back, knowing she'd hit the seed inside.

Francesca cut her way out of the peach. Another Sentient Peach was rolling towards a chef battling away at a third peach.

Leaping down from her perch, Francesca used her carving knife to cut a huge slice off the rolling thing. The splatter of flesh pushed the endangered chef out of the way of both fruits and he pulled out his skewer, running forward in hopes of skewering at least one of the things.

Francesca paused just a moment to orient herself. She breathed hard and it echoed in her ears over the pounding of her heart. She barely heard the screams of her fellow chefs as they were wounded in the battle.

More of the peaches were flooding the bay. It was a battle of men and women in tall rounded white hats and suits against pink, orange, and golden spheres. One of the Sentient Peaches was smaller and so young it still had a stem on it, the green piece of branch keeping it from rolling exactly the way it wanted.

Francesca reached it and carved flesh from its other side, making it even harder for the fruit to move forward. As it was near where the force field had been before the battle had started in earnest, it blocked some of the other peaches from getting inside.

Using her extra-long paring knife, Francesca skewered the young peach. Her second kill.

She moved around the sphere only to be greeted by an even larger peach. This one was nearly red on the side that greeted her, with only a bit of gold at the top and perhaps the other side. It nearly rolled over the smaller, dead Sentient Peach, moving towards Francesca with a speed she wouldn't have believed if she wasn't there seeing it with her eyes.

Before it reached her to roll over her, crushing and suffocating her with its weight, Francesca used the boiling water in her chef's hat to scald the thing. When it was down, another of the chefs rushed up and skewered it with his skewer, just to be sure.

"Fall back!" the order came through her helm.

Francesca had to look around to find which way was back. She slipped and slid, despite her heavy gravity boots, back towards the doors of the bay.

Just beyond, she noted the silver color of one of the long,

narrow cutters, the knife at its tip out and ready to spear anything.

Even the rounded tip of the cutter could destroy peach flesh if it was going fast enough, but coming into the bay, it would have to slow down.

It could mean only one thing. The pilot was going to spill the water tank that held its source of boiling water. It wasn't unlike the chef hats but the cutter ships held more.

Francesca hurried to get out of the way. Her space suit would protect her, but she didn't want to be slowed down and perhaps get rolled over by a dying peach.

The cutter skewered two Sentient Peaches before coming to a stop and spraying the water over them. Some were immediately scalded while most were washed out of the bay.

Other cutters waited. Even the science ship, a cigar-shaped thing with knives along its outside except for the back bay where Francesca fought, could fight. It just wasn't quite as powerful as the battle-kitchen ships, where the bays could be opened to the boiling water below. Only after the first round of peaches were boiled did the chefs go in and start slicing and dicing.

Francesca watched as there were fewer and fewer Sentient Peaches moving. She breathed out a sigh. They had vanquished the fruit.

Francesca and the other chefs had to push some of the dead peaches out so that the other cutters could land. Fortunately, they didn't have to clean the bay. Then she was able to leave and head down the shiny white halls, her gravity boots leaving prints of orange and rose upon the floor. Once she was in an area cleared of damage, Francesca was able to remove her faceplate, the stickiness of it not wanting to let go of her skin.

"We did it!" Head Chef Robert Forth said raising a hand to the other battle chefs.

He gave Francesca a particular smile. "I knew you'd overcome your weightless sickness as soon as you were in a real battle!"

"How did you know?" Francesca asked her boss.

"I had it myself when I was in school. Didn't stop me though. And in those days they needed every trained chef they had. You did good out there. Didn't injure another of your fellows, didn't lose any limbs, and you managed to kill three peaches all on your own."

"Two, I think," Francesca said.

The head chef said no and held up three fingers.

"You'll have dessert for us next week. It will give you time to work up a magical recipe but it won't be so long that you won't still have plenty of flesh to work with," he said.

Francesca beamed. This was her chance. And she had the perfect recipe. She'd been mentally working on it for years, ever since she'd decided to become a battle chef.

Thanks to Head Chef Robert Forth, Francesca had had her big break. Killing the Sentient Peaches was the hard part. Cooking them was easy. Pretty much anyone could do it, but it was the battle chefs who set up their own chains of restaurants who were the leaders in innovation. And now Francesca would be among them.

# THE SLEEPING AGENT
## CHARLOTTE MUNICH

*Charlotte Munich is a fantastically prolific and popular writer in France. She writes great fantasies with strong female characters and a touch of romance mixed in. Sounds mixed up enough to be* Pulphouse Fiction Magazine *material.*

*"The Sleeping Agent" hooked me from the first line and I didn't surface until she let me, just what I love in a great story. This was her first appearance in the magazine.*

# THE SLEEPING AGENT

## CHARLOTTE MUNICH

" S o," the sphinx said, while spreading out the folds of his long purple robe. "What in the Dataverse do you want me to do with that thing?"

He made a frustrated sound and turned his eyes towards the window, as if desperately wanting to escape the conversation. Doug wasn't offended, not really. The sphinx was one of those guys who judged you for anything you undertook, always had a harsh comment for everybody, and never gave anyone more than an ounce of credit. That, Doug's wife thought, was why the sphinx was the sphinx. What would things come to, if the colony was led by someone who didn't show enough authority and determination? Someone too soft, a dreamer like Doug? If Doug was in the sphinx's seat, nobody would do what they were told and everything in Egypt would go haywire in a travel minute, she was certain of that. She seemed to be under the impression that the sphinx was single-handedly holding the whole community together. She was very quick to forget he didn't even do any of the digging.

It had been a radiant spring morning and Doug had gone outside early—as you do, when you're lucky or unlucky enough to have a Finding Place on your allotted piece of land. He'd taken Shrink, the home recording animate, while his wife and kid were still sleeping. Careful not to slam the screen door behind him, he'd stepped out onto the porch to get his tools, his shovel and his big red canvas bag. Then, he'd walked to the edge of the property, the animate following in his wake with this clicking sound that Doug liked to think of as happy.

He was especially fond of that corner, for how close to real nature the context could get. There were possibilities there that even looked a bit like trees, and with the light showering like this, on a very fine spring morning, if you squinted just a little, you could pretend you remembered a river running through a lush forest. It was so glorious, the yearning inside him came to such a hopeful hum, that it almost seemed to him as if the void could be filled. Even Shrink felt it.

"Rich context," it had commented in Shrink-speech, and Doug had smiled in approval.

Sometimes they got along just fine, Shrink and him. Seeing the animate in a good disposition, Doug had asked for a smell-sound combo.

"Can you do Morning Coffee and the News?"

Shrink had obliged and had dug out another piece of context, conjuring up an atmosphere. Even better, he'd picked up on Doug's mood. The Coffee was fire camp coffee, and the News came in radio flavor, crackling softly and interspersed with chirping birds. It was old news, of course, which only made it more poetic. In fact, it was so good that Doug had to close his eyes for a second.

Then, of course, he squared his shoulders under his rough

old cotton shirt, and started digging. Digging was what you did, it was the best thing to do, the *only* thing to do. Digging so the sphinx was happy and the family was fed, digging so the soil would not explode with possibilities.

Sometimes he'd find an old shoe, a can of Spam past its expiration date, or a rotten potato you couldn't even plant. Doug's wife would sigh, purse her lips, and tell him to try and concentrate.

His son would ask, "Why no luck, Daddy?" and Doug would answer uncomfortably, awkwardly shifting from one foot to the other:

"You gotta dig up what the Dataverse sends you, son," while his wife turned away with a disgusted face.

Other days, he'd find a toy, a big scrap of metal, or something else he could sell at the market. His wife and son would go while he slept and come back later with dinner.

Once, he dug up a bottle of wine. They opened it, even if they could have sold it for a fortune at the market. It was quite good, fruity and pungent. They laughed and danced, and the kid had Rainwater ™ with fresh mint. Doug and his wife went to bed early that night, and not because they were tired.

So, yeah, digging could make you feel good. But most of the time, you just did it by sheer habit. Two, three hours in the morning, two hours after your afternoon nap, before family time or settlers games or town assembly.

And of course, there was always a chance you'd find something huge. There were stories, true or false, of hard black stones that had fetched a very handsome price at the market. Or rare objects. A flydar unit. A rainmaker, found once, two towns over—although, that one might have been a hoax.

But Doug knew for a fact that his neighbor Frank had

unearthed a plantigrow, one day, and just by his house, not even at a proper Finding Place. The only sad fact was, the thing hadn't offered Egyptian settings. It wasn't suited for their context. So the nice dream of strawberries, cherries, and avocado had died pretty quickly. Not knowing the technology, Frank hadn't dared keep the thing for himself. He'd brought it to the sphinx and had never heard about it again.

What the authorities always hoped for was data, whatever the form. If you found an old book or animate parts, you were supposed to contact the sphinx *at once.*

But what Doug had found this morning...that didn't really make sense. Once he'd pulled out that strange, richly deco- rated box, and opened it, he'd stayed there for a moment with his mouth hanging open.

The animate had been the one to shake him out of it.

"First analysis of Finding: Category C," it had wheezed.

"What?" Doug had protested.

This didn't look like a Cat C Finding. It looked like some- thing big, earthshakingly big.

"Looking for a Market Price Estimate," the animate had gone on. "Toy. Cat C Doll."

"This isn't a toy," Doug had said.

It didn't look like a toy. It couldn't be a person either. Or maybe a child. But it didn't look like a child. What in Egypt was it then?

With a heavy sigh, Doug had closed the box. He'd loaded it very carefully in his red canvas bag, and he'd brought it here, to the town house. Although, now, seeing the sphinx's dismay and disappointment, he was starting to feel like he'd made a mistake.

But he couldn't very well have left this in the ground and ignored it altogether.

"So tell me how it happened," the sphinx sighed, placing the lid back on the box and looking at Doug down his long nose.

Doug swallowed, and told his story.

"I found the box and opened it. She was inside. I closed the box again and brought it all here as quickly as I could."

It—she—didn't even look like she was dead. Sleeping, maybe. Not rotten or anything. In...how did they say at the market?...pristine condition.

"Where was it?" the sphinx asked.

"At my Finding Place."

"Deep?" There was such distaste on the sphinx's face. Was Doug responsible for causing it? Or the little body he'd dug up?

"Not very," Doug admitted, as if apologizing for his laziness. He didn't dig really deep, ever. He'd figured out long ago there really wasn't a point.

Now he wanted to look at her again.

"May I?" he asked.

The sphinx gestured towards the box, clearly irritated.

It was a sarcophagus, Doug saw it clearly now, but of tiny proportions. Two feet at the most in length. She was so tiny. But she wasn't dead. He couldn't believe that now. She had to be sleeping.

With trembling hands, Doug opened the box. He nearly let the lid clap back down again and only just caught it—now, *that* would have annoyed the sphinx, for sure.

He felt intimidated. Not only was she tiny and inexplicable, she was also *very* pretty.

"She looks like a doll," he murmured before he could prevent himself.

But she wasn't a doll. She was a living thing, this was getting more and more obvious to him now. Silky dark hair, closed eyelids, pale rose petal skin, a pretty white dress. Doug desperately wanted to know what color her eyes were.

For the second time, the sphinx held out a long bony finger and poked the doll in the abdomen, probing, hard. Doug winced and wished he would stop doing that. He was going to hurt her.

"Do you think she came from the stars?" he blurted out.

The sphinx looked at him like he was dirt under his shoe.

"There's nothing in the stars," he reminded Doug.

It was government doctrine, taught at school. It had been proven once and for all that all the things in the Finding Places came from the Dataverse. They were excreted into the contexts through a distribution of portals. There were analogies to make things clearer for the common people who didn't grasp quantum physics so well, like Doug. The Finding Places were the equivalent of pores through which the Dataverse got rid of things or circulated them between contexts. Sometimes things disappeared from a context, just to resurface in the next. Egypt, their home, was one of those multiple contexts. That was all there was to know. There was nothing else. But Doug hadn't listened too well in class and he liked the stories better. The ones with wormholes, black holes, stars, and time travel.

Plus, today, the Dataverse was proving him right. This doll couldn't have been *excreted* like some vulgar bodily garbage. She was too pretty, too delicate for that. She just *had* to come from the stars.

"Leave it all to me," the sphinx sighed, and Doug got very, very still for a second.

Then, very carefully: "I will, sphinx. But first, I want to take her to the infirmary, if it's okay with you. Just to make sure she's all right."

The sphinx shook his head.

"It's not a living thing, Danish."

But Doug resisted.

"Well, sphinx, in that case, there's no harm in taking a short look at her, is there?"

"The Doc doesn't have time for this," the sphinx warned.

"Let me just ask him," Doug insisted. "I'll bring her right back afterwards."

"Please do. And make sure you stop calling it a 'she.' We don't want anybody upstairs to get the idea the colony's got a case of livingness on its hands."

Sometimes digging would make you imagine things. Even normal settlers could get strange ideas. Doug's own neighbors had been sent to get treatment for severe hallucinations a couple of months before. They'd started to tell everyone there were living things trying to get through to their Finding Place. Living things from another context, wearing masks. The sphinx had given a long speech at town assembly, to remind everybody of the basic laws of physics that made this ludicrous theory impossible.

Even though Doug was being difficult, the sphinx obviously still didn't think he possessed enough backbone to create problems. He just dismissed him with a gesture of his hand that expressed authorization, boredom, and threat all in one go. Doug softly closed the box and balanced the canvas

21

bag on a shoulder. The infirmary was in a building just next door.

When he got there, the town physician, Dr. Osiris, was indeed busy. He was embalming a body and joyfully humming to himself.

"Sweet little Mrs. Smackel." He smiled at Doug while extending his gloved hand. Doug didn't shake it, though, preferring to just nod. "She was only ninety, the poor thing."

Other than Mrs. Smackel, the town infirmary was empty that late morning. Settlers were tenacious bastards, as Dr. Osiris liked to remind everybody. Embalming seemed to be the bulk of his practice, or maybe he just enjoyed it the most.

"What's up, Danish?" Dr. Osiris asked Doug.

"I've brought something for you to examine."

He set the sarcophagus on Dr. Osiris's desk and hesitated. He was starting to have second thoughts about this. But since he was there, and Dr. Osiris was growing impatient, no doubt wanting to get back to his embalming party, Doug lifted the lid.

"Oh, my," Dr. Osiris exclaimed. "What is that?"

He didn't poke her. Instead, he started foraging in his tools, soon retrieving a scalpel.

"What are you doing?" Doug cried out, placing himself between the good doctor and the sleeping doll.

"What does it look like?" Osiris asked. "I've never seen something like that. It's of scientific interest that I should examine it."

"Put that scalpel away," Doug growled. "You're going to kill her."

"*She*, as you call that thing, is pretty much dead already, my dear Danish."

But Doug didn't believe that.

"Can't you do an ultrasound instead, or something? Pull out a stethoscope? Something less invasive?"

Reluctantly, the doctor let go of the scalpel and Doug relaxed a little. But then he tensed again. He knew what the ultrasound machine looked like; he remembered it from when his wife was expecting their son. And it was *not* that strange closed cabin that the doctor was now opening.

"Just put her here," Osiris said. "We'll take a look at her heartbeat."

"An ultrasound?" Doug asked carefully.

"Better," Osiris affirmed, but Doug had trouble believing him.

The good doctor looked strange and was starting to sweat in the face.

"I'm sorry," Doug said, "I shouldn't have disturbed you like that in the middle of your day. You clearly have so much to do already. I'll come back later when there's more time, and we can discuss this more comfortably."

"You can leave the box with me," the doctor said agreeably.

But Doug was already closing it and gathering it into his arms like the treasure he was now sure he'd found.

"Danish. Don't do that. It's dangerous," Osiris warned.

"Why?"

Osiris gestured at the samples decorating the walls of his office.

"Germs," he offered.

But he didn't seem convinced. And nobody ever bothered about any germs coming into the context through any of the

Finding Places. You just drank the wine, thanked the Data-verse for the can of Spam even if it was a few weeks past its expiration date, and went on with your life.

"I'll be careful," Doug promised as he exited the infirmary.

———

O n the way back, he decided that he couldn't put the doll back in the cargo and that she would ride with him. He used the decorated box as a cot, just as he'd done with his kid when he was a baby, and secured it to the back seat of his transporter. In this little nook, the doll looked so peaceful.

Shrink started to fuss: "Germ Analysis."

But Doug cut him off sharply. "Stop that or I'll deactivate your analysis functions."

He drove slowly, cautiously. His farm wasn't far out of town. It was merely a ten-minute drive back from the town house.

He stopped in the last curve and parked on the side of the road. It was noon and his stomach was starting to groan. He turned around to look at his passenger. This was where he should consider closing the lid and hiding the box into the back of his truck, so as not to worry his wife and kid. But he couldn't really bring himself to do so.

"What are you? What shall I do with you?" he asked the doll.

"What are you? What shall I do with you?" the doll answered in a melodious voice.

Doug's heart nearly stopped.

"Voice Analysis," Shrink suggested.

"Just record," Doug told the animate, before focusing on the doll.

She was still sleeping peacefully, her dark eyelashes resting their golden tips on her pale pink cheeks.

"What's your name?" he asked the doll.

"What's your name?" the doll replied.

"I'm Doug."

Silence followed, only inhabited by Shrink's recorder whirring. Doug was getting started to speak again when the answer finally came.

"I'm Angst."

"That's a strange name for a girl," Doug laughed.

The doll was quiet and now he was afraid he'd offended her. But he wanted to know more.

"What are you doing here?" he asked.

"What are you doing here?" the doll answered.

"I'm a farmer. I grow stuff and dig my Finding Place. That's where I found you."

"I'm a feeling. I grow tired and draw a Fun Thing. That's how I dreamt you," the doll said.

"Sleeping Toy displaying Mimetic Speech Pattern," Shrink ventured.

But Doug's heart was beating fast. Skipping the question part altogether, he went on.

"I have a wife called Sandy and a kid named Johnny."

"I have a theory called Sorrow and a carol named Joy," the doll said, moving her cherry-pink lips with her eyes still closed.

"I feel sorrow and joy too," Doug approved. "Sorrow makes me sleep and joy makes me sing."

"I date sparrows and tortoises too. Sparrows are so deep,

25

and tortoises come in the spring."

She was so weird.

"Toy," Shrink insisted.

"I don't think so," Doug said to the animate.

"I don't like Poe," the doll added.

This conversation was going nowhere.

"This is a living thing," Doug insisted.

"Biopsy?" the animate asked, wagging its electronic tail in anticipation.

"Are you crazy? No, of course not. Let's bring her home and talk to her some more."

————

D oug's wife, Sandy, wasn't happy.

"What is this thing? She's horrible. She makes my skin crawl."

Doug decided Sandy at least deserved some credit for calling Angst a "she."

"She says her name is Angst. She's a feeling and she dreamt us."

"Well, isn't she just the little poet," Sandy snarled.

"Try talking to her," he advised.

Sandy grimaced, but she knelt by the sofa where Doug had set the box and, with her nose inches away from the doll's, she declared:

"I'm the lady of the house and I don't like trouble."

"I'm a baby from the stars and I don't talk bubble," the doll replied without opening her eyes.

Sandy shrugged.

"Very amusing. Did you dig up something good otherwise this morning?"

"Just Angst here," Doug said.

Sandy looked disappointed.

"What are we going to eat then? Is Angst here going to put food on the table?"

"Where Angst comes from, you can dream up food," Angst offered.

"Well," Sandy snarled, "can you dream up food *now*?"

"Can you dream up food *now*?" Angst mimicked, pissing Sandy off even more.

"Don't talk to her directly," Doug intervened. "She doesn't like that."

Sandy made a disgusted face.

"Don't be mad at the finder," Angst said. "He can't grow like that."

Doug smiled and Sandy threw her hands in the air while Shrink insisted, sniffing at the doll: "Suggested Course of Action: Pattern Analysis. Biopsy. Reclassification from Cat C Toy into Cat A Sleeper Agent. Hazard Code: Red."

"Will you shut up?" Doug told Shrink.

True to his settings, Shrink shut up. But now Doug's son was coming home from school.

"Son! Come take a look at what I found!" Doug exclaimed proudly.

"Go to your room *at once*," came the counter command from the boy's mom.

"Angst, this is Johnny," Doug explained, dismissing his wife's anxiety. "He's learning to read."

"Johnny, I am Angst. I'm brimming with food."

"Brimming?" Johnny asked. "Do you have chocolate?"

"Brimming?" the doll repeated. "Do you have chocolate?"

"Angst doesn't deal with direct questions very well," Doug explained to his son.

"Remind me again what that thing is doing in my house?" Sandy asked.

———

"Doug doesn't feel like snide allusions from hell," Angst intervened.

Doug just hoped his son would see the incredible beauty in today's finding. He wished Angst would just manifest the chocolate necessary to convince Johnny. He tried a new, sideways approach.

"Johnny is hungry and wants to eat chocolate."

"Angst is angry and wants to reap desolate."

This didn't sound too good. Sandy was looking at Shrink, no doubt a second away from calling the sphinx's office and telling Doug off about the doll. Doug made another attempt at talking to Angst. He just couldn't shake that feeling, that they were *communicating*.

"Angst could try and dream up some food," he suggested.

"Doug should try and keep Angst for good," the doll answered.

Sandy was furious now. "We're settlers. We don't have time for games. If you can't put food on the table, you need to go, young lady."

Angst's voice was icy as she replied: "You're beggars. You will have time for games. If you can't get in the mood for battle, you'll feel the blow, sour pussy."

"Is she threatening me?" Sandy exploded. "That's it.

Shrink, call the sphinx *now*. Doug, you should have done this *hours* ago."

The animate started to make this groaning, creaky sound that announced the start of a communication.

"Shrink, don't you dare," Doug growled.

The animate stopped, uncertainly dancing from one foot to the other. It was meant to take orders from the whole household, but in the event of conflicting instructions, it was supposed to listen to Doug first. Except if Doug was exhibiting dangerous or illegal behavior. Then, it was Shrink's call.

"Data Analysis," the animate clicked and whirred, wagging its metallic tail.

"Shrink, quiet," Doug warned.

"Data Suggests Cat A Sleeper Agent Destined for Immediate Elimination," Shrink decided.

"What?"

The animate was equipped with incineration functionalities but wasn't supposed to destroy anything on its own accord. Yet it was marching on Angst while an ominous-looking hose protracted from its hull, demonstrating a behavior that hadn't previously been on its list of options.

"No! Wait!" Doug cried out, throwing himself between the animate and the doll.

"Please Clear Target Course for Immediate Destruction," Shrink warned.

"Shrink! Stop this *now*."

But Shrink was showing no sign of obedience. In fact, it was whirring like crazy, its retractable turret now focusing on Doug.

"Removal of Obstacle," the animate decided.

"Shrink, stop!" Sandy called.

Shrink didn't stop, even when Sandy kicked it in the loco-motion area. That just distracted it from Doug, making Sandy its new preferred target.

"New Obstacle Detected for Immediate Incineration," it warned, aiming at the lady of the house.

"Johnny, go hide somewhere," Doug yelled at his son before running to the porch to get his digging tools. Coming back with his shovel as quickly as he could, he swung it at the animate, hard, hitting the base of the offensive turret.

In an explosion of sparkles, the weapon bent at its base and Shrink's control panels went haywire.

"General Destruction, Brace for Collateral Damage."

"What in the Dataverse?" Sandy yelled.

Doug grabbed her wrist and ran for the door. He just had the time to collect his son on the way. They were jumping from the porch when their house blew off.

Doug was thrown forward in the air and for a second, felt like he was flying. Sandy went airborne too. As he crashed, he just at the last minute remembered he was still clutching his son. He bent around to land on his shoulder and protect the smaller frame. It hurt, but they were otherwise unharmed. They both lay there for a minute, gasping, panting and nearly deaf.

"You all right?" Doug asked Johnny.

The boy nodded.

"Sandy?"

But Sandy gave no answer, so Doug started yelling in terror. "Sandy! Sandy!! *Sandy!!!*"

But then she was standing over him, staring down at him, her hair disheveled and her face full of dirt, smoke every-where behind her. She was saying something, no doubt yelling at him in frustration. He was really surprised when she held out a hand for him to grab, so that he could stand up.

His ears were still ringing. He could catch some of her words, and the rest, he read on her lips.

"I can't believe Shrink turned rogue on us!" she said.

"Sorry for that," Doug grimaced.

"It's not your fault. Sorry about activating…whatever happened there. What in Egypt *was* that?"

Doug shrugged. He was starting to get an idea.

"Shall we complain to the sphinx?" Sandy seemed unsure.

"Let me just take a look inside," Doug said, climbing the porch steps to their destroyed home.

"Be careful!" Sandy called. "Shrink might still be there."

But the animate had exploded, blackening the living room walls, sending shrapnel all over their kitchen area. Shrink's telecom unit had embedded itself into the door frame, and its radiator had landed into the oven, destroying the glass and bending the rack inside it. Anyway, Shrink's parts weren't Doug's chief interest here. He went straight to the sofa.

The doll's sarcophagus had been shredded by the explosion. Doug could see colored pieces of wood burning everywhere. He stepped towards the place where the doll had been lying, his heart thudding in his chest, looking for the bloody remains of a tiny being, not knowing if the need to see what had happened to her could surpass the terror of finding her.

But he didn't find her.

She found *him*.

"Angst would suggest a change in scenery," she said, emerging from behind the sofa.

Her eyes were the deepest blue and she looked very serious. She was also two feet tall in tattered clothes that had once been a pretty white dress.

Doug blinked. "I'm happy you're alive and well. Shall I fetch you some new clothes?"

"I'm groggy, you thrive and you smell," the doll answered. "Shall I fetch you some new clothes?"

"You're strange."

"You're in danger."

That much he could believe, so he just grabbed a couple of essentials from the house—a change of clothes, some water, and his shovel—and they both went back outside to Sandy and Johnny. Mother and son were clinging to one another in front of the destroyed house.

Sandy frowned when her eyes fell on the doll, but her comment wasn't hostile.

"I'm glad you made it," she just said.

The doll gestured towards the house. "I'm sad they burned it."

Both nodded.

"What now?" Sandy asked.

"What now?" Angst asked.

"We need to be careful," Doug started.

"We eat our mouths full," Angst decided, and started walking towards the Finding Place.

For lack of a better idea, the family followed. Angst went past the nice bit of context at the back and stopped in a place where Doug never considered digging, because it looked fragmented and damaged, like scar tissue in the context. He'd never have thought you could dig nice stuff from that place. Yet Angst was pointing to it and commanding:

"Dig, Doug."

"What if the sphinx's men come after what happened to Shrink?" Johnny asked.

Sandy and Doug exchanged a glance. The boy was right.

"Dig," Angst insisted.

Doug started shoveling dirt.

One or two minutes later, they heard a vehicle coming down their dirt road. Several vehicles.

"Quickly," Angst prompted.

"I wish I could help you," the boy said, but there was only one shovel.

A minute later, the vehicles had stopped. They'd arrived at the farm. While digging through the rift in the context, Doug listened to the heavy silence by the house. One minute, two minutes. He was shoveling dirt as fast as he could, and *really* hoping the doll knew what she was doing, because he sure had no idea. And he was starting to find the silence at the farm very strange and ominous.

Someone called from the house: "Danish!"

Sandy shot Doug a worried look, biting her lip, but didn't answer. Her show of confidence gave him more strength as he went on digging, maybe not twice as fast, but still faster.

"Danish!" the masculine voice called again. "Are you all right?"

"Are you all right?" the doll echoed softly.

Johnny put his hand on the doll's dark and curly head.

"Don't worry," he murmured quietly. "It'll all turn out okay."

"Don't hurry. You'll catch the ball in the hay."

———

Doug was waiting for the vehicles to leave the place, but it was probably wishful thinking, considering they'd left the car in front of the house. When the visitors called, they were getting nearer.

"Danish! Sandy! Johnny boy, are you there? Everything okay?"

"Johnny boy, are you there? Everything okay?" the doll had to ask anxiously.

At the same moment, Doug hit pay dirt. With a ringing sound, the shovel hit something hard. A metallic hull, or maybe a stone? He tried looking at it between his feet, but all he could see was that scar in the context. Behind the shimmering pearly veil, he could see only darkness.

"Keep digging," the doll said.

"Where are you taking us?" he asked, forgetting the weird thing with the doll and direct questions. So the answer, unsurprisingly, was disappointing:

"Where are you taking us?"

Doug sighed, but did as he was told.

Meanwhile the town men had stopped calling, but that didn't mean they'd left. The vehicles were still there.

"They're coming towards us," Johnny whispered.

"Dig," the doll said. "Dig to the stars."

Doug froze.

The stars? Did she mean the stars were a real thing, despite everything you were told at school and in life?

But if he dug to the stars, what would happen then?

He swallowed his questions.

"I've always believed in the stars," he said.

"I've always believed in the tsars," Angst answered fervently.

Sandy and Johnny were starting to feel afraid too, he could tell. So he did the only thing he could: dig faster through the glitch in reality, forget everything he thought he knew about the context, and dream, dream up again all the dreams he'd unlearned along the years.

Eyes closed, he went on digging, despite the absurdity of it, but not as a farmer dug.

No, he dug as the dreamer he really was.

"Daddy, it's happening," Johnny said in a whisper.

He still wouldn't open his eyes, for fear of un-happening it. Digging still, he was listening to the dream, smelling something from beyond context, a rich sense of possibilities. A warm feeling was spreading through his belly, and the muscles in his arms and back weren't hurting so badly anymore.

"You're doing it," the doll confirmed.

But then he heard that masculine voice, booming:

"Oh, Danish, here you are. What's with all the secrecy? And the explosion at your house?"

Doug opened his eyes, only to find the sphinx himself standing there. Instead of his purple robes, he was wearing pants and a sweater that looked totally incongruous on his slight frame.

"Oh, hi, sphinx," Sandy smiled brightly. "We're having a family dig."

The colony, after all, encouraged these, even if they rarely ever took place. Digging holes in the dirt, hoping to find something good, was, after all, a tremendously boring pastime, so if you didn't *have* to, it was always best to skip it.

"A family dig, how sweet," the sphinx commented sarcastically. "I didn't know you still did that, Doug. And what's this little person with you?"

His eyes fell to the doll. Angst took a step backwards, perhaps remembering the way the sphinx had poked her just an hour before.

"Yes," Doug said, keeping his nerve, "this is my cousin Angst from out of town, sphinx. She's visiting right now, hence the family dig."

"Oh, I see," the sphinx said.

But out of his pocket, he produced a handgun, one of these weapons only government people could wield.

Now it was Sandy's turn to gasp and recoil.

Doug, though, remained calm. Dreaming something up, whatever it may yet be, had a strangely soothing effect on him, he found. So soothing, in fact, that the dreaming was still taking place within him, even though the sphinx was now threatening his family and their doll with his government-issue gun.

"I'm awfully sorry, sphinx, but I don't think we'll be staying in your context anymore," he said without anger. "We are going to the stars now."

The sphinx should have said there were no stars; it was practically a reflex answer at this point, a leitmotif in their interactions. But he just frowned and shot his gun.

Not at Doug. Not at Sandy. Not at Johnny.

At the doll.

Doug cried: "No!"

The doll fell silently to the ground, but as she fell, she turned around and with a smile, she *winked* at him.

Doug let go of his shovel to grab Sandy and Johnny's

hands. He had to act quick now, before the sphinx shot them all. Squeezing his loved ones' hands in his, he closed his eyes, willing the dream to become true.

And…it did.

Well, at first, opening his eyes, he thought nothing had happened. The sphinx was, after all, standing right before him, his hand extended in front of his body. And the doll, Angst, was gone.

But the sphinx wasn't holding a gun. He was holding a shovel. And it wasn't really the sphinx, seeing as this man was *cheerful* as he greeted them with a big smile.

"Hi, family! Welcome to the Afterworld, the place where digging makes sense!"

Doug and Sandy exchanged a flabbergasted look.

"What? Where's Angst?"

"There's no angst here," the sphinx joyfully replied.

"No…" Johnny said. "You don't understand. The doll!"

"Oh, you mean the sleeper agent? You mean you liked her?"

The sphinx put his fingers to his mouth and whistled loudly.

"Hey, dolly! Come closer."

And there she was. Angst. Two feet tall, alabaster skin with the faintest shot of pink on her cheeks, blue eyes, white dress.

"Can we keep her?" Johnny asked.

"Sure," the other sphinx said. "As long as you keep digging like you just did. Wow, man, that dream was something. It's not every day that we get serious candidates from Egypt. I can't tell you how happy I am."

Maybe Doug should have been happy, but all he felt was revulsion. This was the afterlife? No way.

He took the shovel from the new sphinx and thanked him politely.

"I'll start digging right away. Could my, hum, family dig with me too?"

This threw the sphinx, but he quickly recovered.

"A family dig? How quaint. Sure. Of course. The family that digs together, stays together. Yes. Have at it. Great fun."

He gave them all shovels, then went away.

"Hey, Angst," Doug said to the doll when he'd left. "Sorry you had to die."

Angst smiled and winked a periwinkle-blue eye.

"No problem, boss. Shit happens. What are we doing now?"

Doug thought about it for a second, then said: "We'll be digging our way out of here. I want to take Sandy and Johnny to see the stars. We're going to travel. I don't feel like I truly master this dreaming thing yet. Can you help?"

Angst shrugged.

"Sure, boss. Maybe we need to expand your imagination a little, and get you better expectations in life."

"Yeah," Doug agreed. "Fewer sphinxes, less digging maybe, more stars."

"More chocolate," Johnny added.

"White horses on sandy beaches," Sandy mused.

"You're both naturals," Angst approved. "Let's go."

"Am I really supposed to dig?" Doug asked.

"Well," the doll said, "I'm not going to do it for you, pal."

So Doug started digging, and after a while, Sandy and Johnny came to help him while the doll sat there, telling them strange stories of her long career as a sleeping agent. It was a lovely spring day, and the context, all in all, was much nicer than the old one, with a better sphinx, greener grass, and a river running just yards away, where they could take a break, should the digging not produce immediate results.

So Doug and his family felt very relaxed. They found that, the more relaxed they felt, the more fecund the dig proved. By evening, they'd dug up a castle, a horse, a nice seven-course meal for everyone, and were seriously considering spending the night here before taking off for the stars.

It was a very nice day of digging.

# OBJECTS OF DESIRE

## NINA KIRIKI HOFFMAN

Acclaimed veteran fantasy writer Nina Kiriki Hoffman allowed us to reprint one of the wildest and craziest stories ever written, "Savage Breasts," in Issue Zero of this magazine. In fact, it started off that very first issue.

Nina can not only write fantastically fun fantasy, but she can grab a reader and make them think. I remembered this story from a forgotten out of print paperback anthology called **Alien Pets** way back in the mid-nineties. I had a story in the same anthology and I just didn't want this story of Nina's to vanish any longer. So here it is in this book for a new generation of readers to enjoy.

Nina is a musician, a writing instructor, and a judge for Writers of the Future. And amazingly fun to be around if you get the chance.

# OBJECTS OF DESIRE

## NINA KIRIKI HOFFMAN

E veryone was getting skewlis. I wanted one so much it hurt.

I didn't know about trends. I hated that when three of my friends got black high-top shoes with light-up lightning bolts on them, I wanted my own pair sooo much. I mean, why should I care? It was like some chip in my head switched on and said WANT. It kept digging at me until I whined at Mom.

She used to just give me whatever I wanted, but since her job diminishment, she couldn't afford to do that anymore.

Sometimes she talked to me about worldview, global perspective, how we were small in something giant and we had to work with all the other things to get along okay, and when I listened hard enough, I could shut the WANT chip off.

Sometimes she just said, "Kirby, shut up about it now," but the chip kept sending the WANT message. It was hard to ignore.

So anyway, people at school started showing up with skewlis. Sort of a cross between a weasel and a cat: skewlis

43

had round heads with cute pointy ears and big eyes, slinky arms and legs that wrapped around your arm, and long bodies that bent when your elbow bent. They came in designer colors and patterns like Blue Razzberry and Circuitboard and Seawave. Smart enough to fetch, open cupboards and drawers, learn cute tricks, and accomplish small tasks. Motivated by specially engineered snacks that kept them willing and docile. Guaranteed by the F.P.A. to not be usable as weapons.

Pretty soon most of my friends and a lot of other kids were walking around with skewlis heads on one shoulder or the other, skewlis bodies doubling the width of one arm. People looked like mutants. Honto cool mutants.

The best skewlis brands had tons of max-excellent options. You could computer-blend a color scheme and the company would build you a skewlis to match. You could pick traits like "makes musical noises" or "will act as alarm clock." My friend Pati got one that would hold her bookscreen for her while she read, and press the text-scroll icon when she nodded.

I didn't want a skewlis at first. They were just too weird and creepy.

But after almost everybody I knew got one, I started feeling odd without that extra head on one shoulder, that widening of one arm, that pair of jewel eyes watching everything. I felt deformed.

So when Grandma got me a skewlis for my birthday, I was glad.

My fourteenth birthday party was nothing like my thirteenth birthday party had been. Between this year and last year, Mom lost her big job and had to take little ones, so I couldn't have a huge party and invite tons of friends over.

Mom, Grandma, and I sat around the kitchen table. Mom

had managed to get enough meat for us to have my favorite, beef stew, and Grandma had baked me a small square cake and covered it with strawberry frosting. Which was a great switch from basic rations. No matter what color or shape they made base, it all tasted pretty much like cardboard.

After we ate dinner and the cake and said how great it tasted, I opened my two presents: a new pen with temperature-sensitive skin that changed colors, and a silver shirt with a hologram of my favorite band on the front. Both of these presents were things I really liked. I throttled the little voice inside that whined because I didn't get more. I said a lot of thank-yous and hugged my presents and figured that was it.

Then Grandma brought the carry-cage out from under the table. A faint smell of lemons and incense came from the cage.

She set the carry-cage in front of me.

For a second I couldn't breathe. I knew we couldn't afford what I really wanted. Maybe she had gotten me a kitten. That would be okay. If Mom said it was, anyway. I would need to get extra after-school jobs so I could buy cat food.

I leaned forward and opened the door of the ribbon-wound carry-cage.

The skewlis emerged slowly. At first I thought it was gray, and I felt a flicker of disappointment. At school, people fussed most about skewlis with bright colors: turquoise, cotton-candy pink, acid green with baby-blue stripes. This one looked dull in comparison.

Then light glanced off it, and I saw that it was a soft lavender color. Its huge eyes glowed orange-red. Its front feet looked just like little black hands. It came out onto the table among the tempconfetti and torn gift wrapping, then sat back and stared up at me.

45

I stared back, wondering what it was thinking. What did any pet think confronted with a new owner? I have to spend the rest of my life with you whether I like it or not? Amuse me? Oh, no?

It lifted one small black hand and held it palm outward toward me. Confused, I lifted my own hand in answer and slowly brought it forward.

The skewlis touched its palm to mine. Its hand felt hard and small and hot. My hand tingled around its touch. It made a chirring noise, jumped over my hand, and clamped its arms around my upper arm, bringing its head up beside mine. Its lemony smell grew stronger for a second, then faded. The tip of a pink tongue flicked from its mouth. Its orange eyes stared at my face from unnervingly close.

It weighed almost nothing. The grip of its arms and legs around my arm felt weird for a moment, but then I stopped noticing. I turned to Grandma. "Thank you," I whispered. "Thank you."

"Oh, good," she said. "I hoped you would like it." She hesitated, then said, "It's not one of the famous brands."

Grandma was a veteran bargain hunter. She specialized in factory seconds, reconditioned obsolescence, open box returns, and "that stain is so small no one else will ever notice it, but they knocked five dollars off anyway." I used to think she was funny and irritating about that stuff, but lately I'd been trying to learn how she did it.

The best skewlis on the market had small seven-pointed stars branded onto their hind legs. There were two other acceptable brands, but after that, you got into the gray area of copycat skewlis. Rip-off companies put together inferior versions. I'd heard about near-skewlis fakes and their problems.

I didn't want to think about that on my birthday, when my grandmother had just given me the perfect present.

My skewlis had a brand I'd never seen before, a little blue spiral almost hidden by the silver-lavender fur on its hind leg.

"It's all right," I said.

"It doesn't have any of those fancy features," she continued, looking worried.

"It's great, Grandma," I said. "It's perfect. Thank you." With the skewlis so close to me now, I could see a very faint tiger-stripe pattern in blue over the silvery lavender of its coat. My skewlis looked like a ghost version of others I had seen, and I thought it was really honto neat.

"What will you call him, Kirby?" Mom asked me. Her voice had a familiar edge to it. Grandma had done something important without asking her again. Mom was mad. But it was my birthday, and she didn't want to be the bad guy.

I stroked my finger over the top of the skewlis's head. It closed its eyes and chirred. "Her name is Vespa," I said in a small voice.

Vespa opened her eyes to stare into mine. Her chirrs grew louder. I didn't remember any of my friends' skewlis making noises like this, but it sure made me feel warm and strange.

"Vespa?" Mom said. "You're naming her after a scooter?"

"Huh? I don't know what you mean. It's just her name."

"Oh," she said. She smiled and shook her head.

I looked at Grandma. "Is there a manual? How do I take care of her? What do I feed her?" I thought about the special food my friends fed their skewlis: small soft brown cubes. I wondered how expensive it was. Probably really expensive, the way most designer stuff was. Had Grandma bought some? Was Vespa hungry now?

Grandma licked her lips, looking away from Mom's accusing stare. "There's no manual," she said. "The man I got her from told me she'll eat what humans eat, and she just needs a little box with sand in the bottom to do her duties in. Always give her access to fresh water, and bathe her about once a week with water and baby shampoo. He said...he said she'll teach you what she needs." She reached under the table and brought up a small sack of cat litter and a high-sided plastic tray. "For starters," she said.

"Thanks!"

Vespa rubbed her head against the side of my head. Her fur was exquisitely soft. She smelled so good. Lemon, stick incense, fresh bread.

There wasn't much left of dinner, it had all been so good. I pressed cake crumbs together and held them up in my hand. Vespa reached out, grabbed a handful, and sniffed them, then ate them. She chirped.

"You can keep the carry-cage," Grandma said.

"Thank you, Grandma. It's a terrific present. Thank you." I glanced at Mom. "I'll get more babysitting jobs. I'll make enough money to feed her," I said. "She's so little, I bet it won't take much."

Mom's frown softened. "Oh, Kirby, it's not that."

Whatever it was, I didn't want to hear about it now. I just wanted to be happy for a little while. "Thanks, everybody, for the best presents and a great meal," I said.

I didn't even have to rack the dishes that night. I took my new things up to my room.

I only thought for a little while about the mountain of

presents I had gotten last year when we could afford a big party, when Mom had loved getting me anything I wanted. A lot of those presents were broken and gone now, and a few I had sold so I could get some honto rad school clothes this year instead of the basics that Mom could afford.

I still had my lightning-bolt shoes from last year. Nobody in my class except me wore them anymore, but I still liked them, even though the batteries in the bolts were almost dead and the lightning only flickered when it rained.

It had been kind of weird not following everybody else from one trend to the next since Mom's downgrade. I watched how much I wanted something when all the other kids got it, and I watched how much I didn't want it two or three weeks later when they had moved on to something else. I felt like I was getting this figured out.

Until I got total skewlis envy, no matter how hard I tried to pretend I thought they were creepy and weird.

But so what? Grandma had done it! She'd managed to get a skewlis for me, who knew how! I didn't have to fight my longing anymore.

I glanced at Vespa. Her furry cheek was close to mine. She scanned my bedroom with fire-orange eyes. Warmth spread through me.

What if everybody had already moved on from skewlis to something else? What if, when I got to school tomorrow morning, I was the only one with a skewlis?

Vespa turned and stared into my eyes. I remembered how much I had wanted a skewlis, even though I knew there was no way. This time I didn't want my wanting to fade. I had Vespa. I needed to keep on wanting her, for both our sakes.

She reached out a tiny black hand and patted my cheek.

Her fingers were warm. She grasped my earlobe, stared at it, and muttered small sounds more like bird-chirps than purrs. My throat tightened for a moment. I felt amazingly happy.

I filled a cup with water in the bathroom and showed it to Vespa. She jumped down off my shoulder and drank three cups full. I also set up the litter box and showed it to her. She stared at it for a long moment, then looked at me sideways. I wasn't sure what to think. What if she had never used a litter box before? Was she even housebroken?

Oh well, deal with that tomorrow, if I had to.

Vespa jumped up onto my right arm. I patted my left shoulder, and after a moment she crept across my shoulders and locked onto my left arm. I cleaned my teeth and washed my face right-handed, with her still clinging to me. I wondered how we would sleep, or how I'd even change into the mega T-shirt I slept in.

But she responded when I patted the bed: jumped down off my arm and curled up, watching me change into my T-shirt. I went into the closet to hang up my clothes, though, and the instant I was out of her sight she made loud beeping/clicking noises that sounded sort of like a burglar alarm. I ducked back into the room and stared at her.

"Che, che," she scolded, reaching one hand out to me and frowning with her eyebrows. She looked like the ruler of the world.

Did all skewlis act like this? I wished I had documentation. Or that I could go downstairs and log on and look for information. But I didn't want to walk in on Mom and Grandma fighting.

I could ask people at school tomorrow.

I slid under the covers and waved the light out. A second

later it lit again. Vespa held her hand out to it. She stared at the light for a moment, then looked at me. Her eyes looked spooky with the light coming from the side; small green moons floated in their centers.

Then she bounded up the bed until she was on the pillow next to my head. She held up her arm and waved the "lights-out" signal, and my room darkened.

I listened to her breathing, smelled her lemon-and-fresh-bread scent. I felt keyed up. I couldn't remember how smart my friends' skewlis had been. Could a skewlis figure out complicated cause-and-effect from just seeing it once? Maybe Vespa had learned that light-switch trick somewhere else.

She purred.

I'd heard skewlis make all kinds of noises. I'd never heard one purr before. Before I could consider that, though, I got sleepy. The purring sounded so fine and reassuring. Like, "All's right with the world."

---

I opened my eyes the next morning and felt Vespa's hands on my forehead. She let go a second later, so I wondered if I had dreamed it.

When I went into the closet to get my school clothes, she followed me in. She clasped her arms and legs around my leg, scolding at me. I wondered if I was going to like close attention in such big doses.

Vespa shared my breakfast bars with me, and took a sip of juice concentrate.

What was I going to do about the litter box situation at school? Maybe somebody would explain it to me.

In the halls before school started, skewlis were still every-where. My friend Pati rushed up to me and complimented me on Vespa. I looked at her baby-blue-eyed, pink-and-green-checked skewlis (named Ramtha) and realized I liked Vespa's coloring much better. Not that I said anything about it. Other friends gathered around and stared at Vespa, checked her brand, nodded to me as if I'd managed to squeak into their club.

I noticed five or six kids in the hall with black buttons big as hands on their jackets. Colored letters, kana, and Sanskrit flashed across the buttons, not making words, just pulling at my eyes.

"Oooo," said Pati, and raced off to inspect one of the buttons.

I noticed the kids with buttons didn't have skewlis. *Well. The Next Hot Thing is here,* I thought.

Vespa patted my forehead. I didn't remember other skewlis doing that to anybody.

But it was strange. The WANT chip had switched on in my brain as soon as Pati ran away to look at buttons, even though I thought I had killed that chip by getting Vespa. I mean. I really thought I had killed that damned chip. What could be better than Vespa?

Stupid black buttons that didn't even make words?

I saw Rico smile as two girls asked him about his flashing button.

Vespa patted my forehead.

And the WANT chip switched off.

It was just school, and I hadn't done all my homework yet because I had celebrated my birthday by not making myself do the subjects I hated. I ignored the bright new buttons and plowed past everybody to get to study hall.

---

After school Pati and Arco and I walked through the downtown maximall, window-shopping. Pati and Arco went into Everything Matters to look for belts. I didn't go inside. I love that store so much. I always see stuff I want, want, want and can't afford. It's easier for me to just stay out of it and not know what I'm missing. So I wandered over and looked at the food court instead, which was also not a good idea. Vespa and I had shared three lunch bars, and I wasn't hungry at all. But I saw a creampuff with chocolate on top. WANT.

Vespa patted my forehead.

Unwant.

Even though I could almost taste that creamy filling, the flaky, buttery pastry, the cold, hard, bittersweet chocolate shell...

Vespa patted my forehead again, and I stopped craving.

---

Dazed, I wandered into Everything Matters. Glass earrings with little eyeballs in them. Pendants made of splattersteel, jingling and throwing off light. Shoe gewgaws with colored gems all over them. The latest in cutaway gloves. Dice chains, fake eyebrow and nose piercings, and a whole row of wide leather belts with small copper and steel shapes grommeted to them.

WANT.

Pat, pat. Unwant.

"Look," Pati cried, showing me a belt. Gold weave with green gems.

"Pretty," I said as she twisted it around her waist. Her skewlis clung to her arm, but didn't seem to be paying attention.

"No, really," Pati said. "Do you think it's me?"

"It's so you," Arco said. "Ja? What about this?"

She held up a scarf with concentric black and red circles on it, then twisted it around her orange-streaked blond hair. "Moi?" Her butter-yellow, tiger-striped skewlis seemed passive too.

"Def," Pati said.

Last time I had come in here with Pati and Arco and a couple other girls I had been so jealous of their credit ratings I couldn't think straight.

I narrowed my eyes and studied Arco. "Not," I said. "So not."

"Honto?" Arco said.

"Too down," I said. It did darken her whole look. "You're an up girl."

"Huh," said Arco. She put the scarf back.

She and Pati experimented with other things in the store. I watched, feeling Vespa's hand on my forehead every once in a while, almost before I knew I was getting sick with wanting again. The want kept going away. I felt a little dizzy and strangely good.

I went outside and over to the window of the leather store. There was a baby-blue suede jacket I had been craving for two weeks. I stared at it and felt nothing, even though Vespa didn't touch my forehead.

I had to sit down.

What was my skewlis doing to me?

I glanced at her. Her head turned as she watched people go by. She seemed fascinated by everything.

I watched too. Lots of people had skewlis grafted to their arms. Most of the skewlis looked tranced or dazed or asleep. None of them patted their people's foreheads. They just looked like...accessories.

"What are you?" I whispered to Vespa.

Her orange eyes stared into mine for a long moment.

Then Pati and Arco came out of the store, loaded down with plastic shimmer bags full of stuff. "Let's get pastry!" Arco said, and we went to the food court.

Pati treated me. She'd been doing that since Mom's diminishment. She never said anything about it. She was a good friend.

I gave Vespa a chunk of my brownie.

"Ack!" Pati said. "You're not supposed to do that!"

"Huh?"

"You're never, ever supposed to give them human food," she said. "It kills them."

Vespa ate her piece of brownie in three small neat bites, then licked her delicate black fingers and looked at Pati.

I said, "I didn't get any documentation. Grandma said she was supposed to eat human food. That's all I've fed her, and she hasn't died yet."

Arco shook her head. "That's so wrong. First thing in the manual is a great big warning to never feed them anything but their cubes."

She broke off a piece of her raspberry doughnut and

offered it to her skewlis, who gasped and shook its head. "Yours is weird," Arco said.

I stroked my hand down Vespa's back.

I knew she was weird.

I just didn't know how or why.

"I mean," Pati said. "Not that she isn't neat, or anything." Her face said one thing while her mouth said another.

"I like her a lot," I said.

Both my friends looked glum and uncomfortable.

Oh no, I thought. Not now.

They had stuck by me when Mom diminished. Pati even loaned me stuff that wasn't the latest, but was the next latest, so I wasn't too far behind and people weren't ashamed to be with me. Was my in-ness going to disappear just because my friends thought my pet was strange?

Vespa touched my forehead and I relaxed. Why want? Why fight? It would be all right.

"Eww," said Arco. "It keeps doing that."

"I like it," I said. Though I wasn't sure I did.

Arco's eyes narrowed a fraction. I felt her going away from me. It made me feel dizzy. Like she was on a motorcycle, looking back over her shoulder, and I was standing in the road. I would never catch up again.

I checked Pati to see if she was going away too. She smiled. "Maybe she's the new, improved kind."

I tapped the table with my free hand and Vespa dropped off my arm. She sat on the table in front of me and looked up into my eyes.

"Eww," said Arco. "You let her on the table? That you eat off of?"

"Huh?" There was so much I didn't know about skewlis

care. I thought back to the scene in the cafeteria at lunchtime. People still wore their skewlis. In fact, the skewlis acted kind of like clothes, even in gym class. People ate with them on, did track with them on, played tennis and baseball.... *I mean*. What was wrong with having them on the table, if they spent so much time on your arm? How different in cootie closeness was that?

I looked around. People at neighboring tables had skewlis. But the skewlis stayed on their arms even as they talked, gestured, used chopsticks or forks or spoons. What was the difference whether the skewlis was on your arm or on the table? I couldn't figure out Arco's distaste. And then I realized.

Nobody else took their skewlis off where you could see it.

I tapped my left shoulder, and Vespa climbed up to lock herself on my left arm.

"She's..." Arco said. Her face pinched into a thoughtful frown. "She thinks too much." She shuddered, her yellow skewlis riding it out with flat, uncomprehending eyes.

Vespa blinked and looked down.

The rest of the afternoon she acted like all the other skewlis I could see.

Dumb.

When we got home, though, we could be alone. Mom and Grandma were still out. I sat down in the kitchen where no trace of last night's party remained. I tapped the table, and, after a glance at me, Vespa dropped down.

Grandma and her bargain-sniffing ability. Huh.

"You're not really a skewlis, are you?" I asked.

Vespa wandered across the table, glancing at the salt and pepper shakers. She touched the napkin holder, then paced around the edge of the table and ended up in front of me, exchanging gazes.

Finally she shook her head.

"Not really a skewlis," I said again. "What are you?"

She sat. She patted the table in front of her with one little black hand. Confused, I stared for a minute. Then I put my hand palm up on the table.

She put her hand palm to palm with mine, and I felt a strange tingling again.

Then it was like she talked to me, but not with words, exactly.

*You're my test*, she told me.

"Your test?"

*My...experiment. My...guinea pig.*

I felt totally creeped out then. My skin crawled. The hairs on my arms stood up. Every mad scientist movie I'd ever seen started playing in my head at the same time. "It's alive. ALIVE!"

Vespa tapped my palm. I shuddered and shook my head, then stared at her. She was just some weird little animal, not a mad scientist. Just some kind of computer glitch, probably, a rip-off skewlis whose dealer prep had misfired.

It was hard to believe that when she looked so...smart. Perfect. Not wrong.

It had to be something else. But what?

Maybe she was someone's experiment too.

She set her palm to mine again, and I stilled. *You're driven so by want*, she said.

Well, yeah, I thought. Duh.

*All of you.*

Everyone? It wasn't just me tortured and sliced open by

wanting all these things that I usually couldn't get? I thought about Pati racing over to look at someone's shiny button that morning. I bet she knew by now where you could buy those things. She would have her own soon. Then maybe she'd stop wanting.

I was so sure. Of course she wouldn't. There would be the Next Hot Thing.

I licked my upper lip. "Okay," I said. "Let me get this straight. You're experimenting on me?" Silly. Idiotic. Scary, even.

She nodded.

"Like, how?" Not that I believed this for a second.

*What happens to you when you don't have to want?*

Sometimes I made myself sick, wanting things so much.

Today I had walked through Everything Matters, and I'd managed not to want anything in there.

With Vespa patting my forehead, anyway.

Everything in Everything Matters was sooo cool, sooo essential. Yet I didn't actually need any of it.

"What happens to me when I don't have to want?" I wondered out loud.

*I don't know yet. Maybe…*

Before she finished that thought, she snatched her hand out of mine. But I'd seen a swirl of strange pictures and thoughts. Earth from space. The bridge of a spaceship, or close enough, anyway, with lots of small blob-shaped people talking to each other and studying TV programs coming from Earth. An intense fear that these wanting people would want so much they would force themselves into space, searching for some elusive thing that wouldn't satisfy them long.

They would boil into space, these Earth people, scorching everything before them and leaving smoke and ash behind.

Unless.

Unless they could be taught not to want so fiercely.

Who would they be if that one thing changed?

Why not find out?

"Stay here," I said, jumping up. I ran upstairs to my room and locked the door. Then I wrapped myself in a blanket and curled up in a corner to brood.

Kind of disgusting to think I was just some dumb rat in someone's maze. With, like, electrodes attached to my brain, zap, teach you not to have that impulse, zap, run this way, that way, zap, oops! Ha ha ha, let's get another rat.

Maybe this was just another thing that had happened because of Mom's diminishment. Only people with no money got bargain basement skewlis, which turned out to be alien mad scientists instead.

But Vespa was so much neater than all the other skewlis.

Sure. And she was playing with my mind. Stinging me in my want.

When I didn't really want to want things so much anyway.

Could she make it stop hurting?

But Arco thought it was weird that she patted my head. If she kept doing it, maybe I'd lose all my friends.

Maybe I wouldn't care, because I wouldn't want friends.

Ewwwww.

Maybe I'd turn into some kind of robot! Or a walking vegetable. Or just a giant chicken. Buck buck. Or a cow. Chew, chew, chew, moo.

Maybe I'd be happy.

Maybe I'd change into someone else completely.

Would that be so bad?

I thought for a while longer, then wrote myself a note.

*DO YOU WANT TO GET OUT OF BED IN THE MORNING?*

*IF YOU DON'T, STOP THE EXPERIMENT.*

I taped it to the ceiling over my bed, then went downstairs.

Vespa was still sitting on the kitchen table, hugging herself. She looked really worried. Not something I'd ever seen a skewlis do before.

I sat down in front of her, took a deep breath, let it out. "Here's what I want," I said. Then laughed. I started over. "What if this turns me into some kind of walking zombie? I don't want to be a walking zombie! I don't want to be dumber than I already am. I don't want to be a...a ghost or an empty person. Do you understand that?"

She nodded.

"I'd kind of like to find out what happens with this experiment too," I said. "But what if it turns out to be a diminishment? I'm scared."

She looked away for a moment, then turned back and nodded.

"If it's just turning me into some stupid goomer, I want you to stop and make it go backward! Can you do that?"

She closed her eyes and hunched her shoulders. She made some little thinking noises. She shifted from side to side.

Then she opened her eyes. She tapped the tabletop with her hand. I put my hand on the table, and she touched my palm.

*I can't guarantee I can return you to a pre-change state.*

My mind startled up. Oh no. Forget it. Tell her to leave right now. She can find another rat.

*It might already be too late for that.*

But—huh? I didn't feel changed at all yet. I checked. I was still totally Kirby. As far as I could tell.

*I will promise to stop whenever you ask me to,* Vespa thought, *and do my best to put wants back inside. You'll still be a little different.*

I took some deep breaths and let them out slowly. This was about the rest of my life. Even if we stopped tomorrow.

After a minute, I said, "Let's do it."

---

So it's been about a week.

So far what I notice is that it's easier to think. I'm not looking around all the time, distracting myself with thoughts about what I can't have.

I can still rent videos and choose clothes. I still hate green basic rations. I can still think about all the feelings I connect with wanting stuff and not being able to have it. I don't know. It's weird.

Everything happens in tiny pieces. I don't know if I'll know when to stop.

Maybe I won't care.

# POWER CHORDS

## BRIGID COLLINS

Professional writer Brigid Collins sells her fiction to all sorts of places. And she sometimes, with her dad, is a guest editor for Fiction River. In fact, she is doing that again this year.

In this original story, Brigid takes her love of music and gives us a fascinating and fun story of aliens and music. A perfect Pulphouse story.

# POWER CHORDS

BRIGID COLLINS

Emma Carlton was reveling in the pure noise energy brewing between her and her guitar, marveling at the nimbleness of her own fingers on the fretboard, shivering at the gritty growl of the new distortion pedal she'd picked up at work yesterday, and most of all, thanking absolute fuck that her crotchety old neighbor Mrs. Sweeny was out of town so she could turn her amp all the way up without worrying about getting another noise complaint hurled at her.

She was sweating buckets, due to either the stifling corn-field-scented summer heat wafting in through the open garage bay door or the way she was throwing herself around and kicking at her equipment while she played, pretending she was Frank Iero at a high-octane concert—and with the new pedal, she almost had the sound right. She couldn't play as fast as him yet, but she was getting there.

Her blood sang in her veins, salt and garage grit coated her lips, her drenched-through tank top and short-shorts were slicked to her like a second skin, and the distorted chords poured out of her, via the guitar, and out into the orangey pink of early dusk.

She was *rocking*.

She was rocking, and for this one evening, no one could stop her. *Nothing* could stop her.

And then the space junk crashed through the garage roof and crushed her amp to smithereens.

"What the *fuck?!*"

Her heart, which had already been racing with the euphoria of playing, started pounding double-time. She leapt backward in reflex, landed on her foot wrong, and went crashing to the dirty concrete floor. Her guitar let out an unamplified and totally un-hardcore squawk.

Her tailbone throbbing, she struggled to sit up and disentangle herself from the guitar strap.

There was a whole bunch more dust in the air now, as well as bits of wood and shingle from the hole in the roof. A smell of singed stone filled the garage. A metallic ticking sound, like an engine cooling off, came from the middle of the floor, right where she'd had her amp situated.

Blinking grit and sweat from her eyes, Emma forced herself to take in the sight of the culprit: a twisted hunk of machinery the size of a mini-fridge embedded in the poured concrete floor. Little wisps of gray-white smoke curled up from it like the trails from incense sticks. The tangled power cords of her amp/pedal setup were splayed outward from under it like the legs of a huge, splatted spider.

"Aw, goddammit," Emma said. She set her guitar aside with arms that shook, then hauled herself over to inspect the damage.

"It's the fucking Russians, I just bet," she muttered. "Spy

68

satellites peeking in on their little social experiment. Fucking guys think they own the country already. Think they can smash my goddamned amp and get away with it? I paid a lot of fucking *money* for that amp!"

By the end, her muttering had become shouting, and her inspection of the space junk with which the Russians had bull's-eyed her amp had turned into flipping double fingers up at the hole in her roof.

Chest heaving, arms shaking, Emma glared through that hole and just *wished* she could develop laser beam eyes right on the spot.

She didn't manage to shoot lasers from her eyes, but she did zero in on the trail of black smoke slowly spreading in the sky. She noticed, now that her guitar had been fucking *silenced*, a thin whistling sound, like a teakettle under the Doppler effect.

She followed the line of the smoke and turned to look out the garage door. Something was hurtling towards the cornfield across the way, giving off that teakettle shriek and spewing black smoke. As she watched, the object struck somewhere in the middle of the cornfield. A faint tremor under her feet followed.

"We'll just go take a little look-see, then," she said. She scooped her phone up from the wooden step leading up into the house and stomped down the driveway. "Get all sorts of photographic evidence, won't we?"

She supposed she should be weeping tears of sweet relief that the space junk had missed her car. She could afford another amp, and fixing the garage roof wouldn't be too difficult, but she couldn't have her car out of commission, or worse, totally destroyed. So she was lucky, really.

But she couldn't get the anger to flush out of her system. Every freaking way she turned, *something* was always trying to stop her from *rocking* it. Whether it was her parents with their stuffy ideas of turning her into a philharmonic player like them (what kid wants to admit she'd had ten years of fucking *harp* lessons?), her so-called friends who'd kicked her out of the band *she'd started*, goddammit (so *what* if she'd insisted they play nothing much other than every song MCR had ever written), or her only neighbor on this lonely stretch of farm road constantly calling the cops on her solo jam sessions (and why the fuck couldn't Mrs. Sweeny just take out her goddamned hearing aids, huh?), it all amounted to the same story. She wouldn't be surprised at this point if her landlord decided to blame the damage to the garage on her hardcore musical aspirations.

She was so sick of it. The goddamned Russians, or whoever was responsible here, were going to pay for this.

"Fucking wreck our country if you can, assholes, but you're buying me a fancy-ass new amp and a whole slew of pedals, and definitely that gorgeous new Fender I saw in Indy last month. That is fucking *happening*."

She crashed through the stalks of not-quite-ripe corn, spelling out more demands for restitution and snapping pictures of the smoke trail with her phone for documentation purposes, and didn't once think of the cliché of aliens in cornfields.

Not, that is, until she reached the crash site.

Even then, *aliens* weren't the first thing she thought of. The first thing she thought was that someone was playing a very cruel, very *weird* joke on her.

Standing in the middle of the cornfield was a harp. A full-size symphony harp, the exact kind she'd toiled away on for ten horrible years under her parents' strict gaze.

Of course, the harp wasn't the only thing in the field. Sitting on a bed of flattened and charred cornstalks was a thing that looked like a Greyhound bus, only with the fortification of a battleship and with no wheels that Emma could see. Its front end had driven itself into the ground, and though the dirt was churned up and plenty of corn had been uprooted, the vehicle itself showed little in the way of crumpling. Most of the damage seemed to have been done to the back end, which had been torn or blasted off. There were scorch marks running along the body, and the stink of burnt metal overrode the sweet corn scent. Emma covered her mouth and nose with the crook of her elbow.

"The *actual* fuck?" she said.

And that was when the harp moved, when it turned to point its sound box at her and crawled towards her on whip-like strings that whispered and zipped against the cornstalks.

<Play me, oh play me quick,> said a melodious, frantic voice in Emma's head.

Emma screamed, tried to run back the way she'd come, got her feet tangled in cornstalks, and went down with a jarring flump. Her phone bounced out of her hand and out of reach. Her teeth clacked together painfully.

For a couple dizzy breaths, she fully believed she'd imagined the whole thing. She had to've.

<Play me, quick! Before *they* come.>

That voice resonated in Emma's head just as if she had that sound box against her shoulder, right next to her ear. And if the voice itself didn't chase away her imagination theory, the

71

harp strings winding around her ankles and shoulders sure as fuck did.

"Oh God oh God oh God," she chanted, struggling. This was it. Death in a cornfield, strung up by a space alien that had taken the form of her old musical nemesis. Fucking shit. When she'd screamed at her mom that she'd rather die than play the harp anymore, she hadn't meant *this*.

<Stop that wriggling and *play me*,> said the harp. <Or do you want to suffer the Silence from Space descending upon your ridiculous planet?>

The strings entwined around Emma's arms and legs lifted her from the dirt and turned her to face the harp. Emma stared at it with wide eyes. Strange, but she couldn't shake the feeling that there was a… a face, or at least eyes, staring back at her from the top of the sound box, right where the curved neck became the shoulder. It wasn't that there was anything carved or painted on the wood there, or that the grain had knots that formed an optical illusion. It was just a feeling she couldn't shake.

Emma realized that the harp had set her down, firmly but gently, on her feet. The strings were unwinding themselves from her, but slowly, as if the harp was ensuring she wasn't about to bolt the moment she had her freedom.

*Not a freaking bad idea,* Emma thought.

But when the strings had receded enough to let the blood rush back into her extremities, Emma held her place.

"You creamed my fucking amp," she said. The anger was running through her blood again, tingling in her fingers and her toes. "What'd you have to go and crash-land on my planet for, anyway?"

72

<Please,> the harp said. <I'm sorry. I can't drive the tour-ship by myself, but my friends are... all my friends are—>

The harp cut itself off. It didn't move, but Emma got the impression its gaze had shifted back towards the smouldering wreckage of the bus thing. Emma cut her eyes that way, too, watching the smoke grow blacker in the deepening evening. A sudden lump formed in her throat.

Oh, Christ. She was feeling sorry for a harp.

<The Silence from Space is following me. If they discover me, if the scouts that are chasing me find this planet, they will descend and devour everything that makes music. Your world will become one of the Damped. It may already be too late.>

Emma rubbed at her prickling arms. Suddenly, this Indiana cornfield was leached of its summer warmth. A world without music? "Oh, fuck no. *That's* not happening."

<Then play me. The computer on the tourship told me I'd find someone at these coordinates who was compatible. It must be you.>

"It's me," Emma agreed, though the words tasted sour. "I guess those ten years weren't for nothing after all."

The harp whipped a string out towards the wreckage and brought a piece of debris over for Emma to sit on. The metal was still hot, but not hot enough to burn the bare skin of the back of her thighs, just enough to be uncomfortably warm through her short-shorts. Once Emma was seated, the harp balanced itself awkwardly on her shoulder.

Her fingers found their places on the strings. A shudder of rebellious revulsion worked its way through her. The harp wobbled a little.

"Okay, what should I play?"

<Anything. Don't worry about being fancy, just be— oh, no.>

Emma felt the harp tense up. Unable to stop herself, she looked up.

Against the deep purple sky to the east, a long, yellowish shape was moving towards them.

<The Silence from Space,> moaned the harp. <We're too late.>

The yellowish shape came on fast. In the space of a down beat, Emma could make out angular details, metallic doohickeys, and what was possibly an array of ray guns that marked it as a spaceship. In two fast measures, the ship was nosing its way straight for their little crash site in the cornfield.

<It's over,> said the harp as the Silence from Space landed their snot-colored spaceship beside them in a whirlwind that set Emma's ponytail flailing. The melodic tones in Emma's head grew ragged with sobs. <They'll Damp us like they did my friends.>

Emma thumped the harp's sound box with the heel of her hand. "Stop that. Jesus, and you called *my* planet ridiculous. Are you going to just roll over and let them do you like that? Are you going to let them get away with what they did to your friends?"

The harp hiccupped. <N-no...>

"When the crotchety neighbors of the universe call in a noise complaint on us, what do we do?"

The harp hiccupped again. <Play... louder?>

"That's fucking right, we do. We play until their ears bleed or our fingers do. Whichever comes second."

The spaceship's door opened with a hydraulic hiss straight out of every alien invasion movie Emma had ever seen. There was even billowing white smoke coming from inside. Any moment now, the BEAs would come shambling out, point their ray guns at her and command her to take them to her leader.

Setting her fingers firmly back on the harp's strings, Emma searched her brain for a harp piece to play, any harp piece, but all she came up with was *the* piece, the one she'd finally quit playing the harp over: a boring, stilted thing her mom in particular had insisted she master. She'd sworn she would never play that one again as long as she lived. *"Not even if I were dying and the only way to save my life was to play it,"* she'd told her mom.

And here she was, in a situation that sure looked a lot like life or death—two shadowy figures were materializing in the smoke-filled spaceship door, and Emma thought she could make out those ray guns held at waist-level. Damping guns, she supposed they were. If there was no more music in the world after this encounter, it might as well be death.

"RrrrrTime to be quiet," said one of the beings descending from the spaceship. Now that it had emerged from the smoke, its wrinkled, leathery green skin was visible, as well as its huge, clearly sensitive ears. The ears were bigger than an elephant's, and they flapped and flared like gills on a fish gasping for air in the bottom of a boat.

The big-eared scout raised its Damping gun and pointed it at Emma's head.

Luckily, Emma had just realized she could play whatever the fuck she wanted right now.

"Eat my riffs, dickweed," she said, and played the first song she'd taught herself to play on the guitar: "I'm Not Okay (I Promise)" by My Chemical Romance.

It sounded off. as. *fuck*. The harp was horribly out of tune, probably due to the crash landing. Not to mention it was a fucking *harp* when this song deserved to be played on an electric guitar distorted all the way to the sweet spot. She missed a lot of notes in the transition between instruments.

But fucking God, it was the most amazing run through of it she'd ever played. She could feel the uncanny liveliness of the strings, the way they breathed, the way the harp undeniably had a mind of its own. She felt the harp rising to meet her halfway on the song, even though it clearly hadn't heard anything quite like emo music before. She'd never had a guitar this in sync with her. Together, they shredded.

"Arrrrrgh!"

The scout dropped the gun to clap both hands over its ears, but its hands weren't big enough for the job. The other scout stepped forward, his own gun held steady.

"RrrrI told you not to take yourrrrr prrrrrrrotective muffs off, rrrrridiot," it said. Its own ears were covered with a pair of the hugest, fluffiest, neon pinkest earmuffs Emma had ever seen. And that was including the time she'd seen Mrs. Sweeny out trying to shovel her own driveway last winter.

The second scout levelled its Damping gun at the harp.

Emma stopped playing. There were times when even the loudest rock 'n roll needed a few measures of silence. For effect.

"Rrrrrthat's morrrre like it," said the second scout. It stomped closer to Emma, keeping the Damping gun held out.

She let him come closer, closer, just a little bit closer, letting those measures of silence stretch and stretch until...

"Frank Iero kick!" she shouted, letting loose with her foot at the same time as she struck her furious down beat. The gun went flying out of the scout's hands and disappeared somewhere in the stalks of corn.

The scout let out a rrrolling squawk of protest and staggered backwards.

"Harp, can you do your string walk while we're rocking it?" she shouted over the music.

<I think so.>

"Then let's *jam*, baby."

Emma kicked the debris she'd been using for a stool away and started using the space of the crash site as her own rock stage, jumping around just the way Frank Iero would. The harp crawled on its strings with her as she moved with the music, flailing and head banging with every power chord she fired out into the night. Wherever the two scouts popped up in the darkness to try to shoot either Emma or the harp, they jammed their way over there and either kicked or stringed the Damping guns away again.

Finally, the harp managed to hook a string around the one scout's pair of earmuffs and rip them away, setting the scout howling under their musical barrage and running for the cover of its ship.

"Nice work," Emma said.

<This is for what you did to my friends!> the harp shouted after the fleeing scout.

But the hydraulic door was closing, and the ship was lifting off. They probably didn't hear the harp's final call.

<That's not good,> said the harp as the two of them watched the booger ship shoot off into the night sky. <They'll send for reinforcements, and the real invasion will begin. I'm so sorry I brought them to your home, but thank you for helping me fight them off this time.>

"No sweat," Emma said, arming a generous beading of the stuff from her forehead. "We'll find some way to send them packing when they show up next time. That was the sweetest jam session I've ever played. I'd started to think I wasn't made for playing with other people after my band cut me out, but I'd actually really missed it."

<I also enjoy playing with others. Would you continue to work with me as I repair my ship?>

"Sure thing. I—"

Something rustled in the corn nearby. Emma tensed, not sure what she should expect after her evening of battle of the space bands.

The first scout came stumbling back into the crash site, holding its ears bundled against its head and looking side-to-side.

"Rrrrroh, that jerrrrk! He rrrrleft me herrrre. He… he… rrrrhe *ditched* me!"

To Emma's surprise, the scout flopped onto the ground and began to cry some of the shrillest, most heartbroken sobs she'd ever heard this side of a toddler. She was almost tempted to cover her own ears. She didn't, though. Instead, she went over and crouched in the dirt beside the scout.

"Hey, uh. It's not so bad. That guy didn't deserve you, anyway," she said. "You could hang with us if you want."

The scout blinked up at her. "RrrrBut I trrrrried to Damp you."

Emma shrugged. "You won't try again, will you?"

"Rrrrnooo…"

"Cool. Wanna join our band?"

The scout blinked again, harder this time. "Rrrrjoin yourrrr *band?*"

<Join *our* band?> said the harp, sounding affronted. <She helped Damp my friends!>

"But she's got a real pair of lungs on her, and a great growly voice that'll do a fucking number on some metal lyrics. If we get her some super sound-cancelling headphones, I'll bet she can sing with us without hurting her ears."

The scout had stopped crying now. "Rrrrthat sounds… fun? RrrrI've neverrrr been in a band beforrrre. Rrrrno one everrrr asked me to join."

Emma clapped a hand on the scout's shoulder, then turned back to the harp. "Come on, Harp. We can't very well defend my home planet from the invasion of the Silence from Space without a vocalist in the group, right?"

<I… suppose not.>

"Then we'll all work together here. Gotta make some compromises if we wanna protect the planet. Peace, love, and punk rock, am I right, or am I fucking right?"

<You're fucking right, I suppose.>

The scout nodded, letting her ears unfurl. "You're fucking right."

Emma pumped her fist in the air. "That's god*damn* right."

Nobody, not her parents, not her cranky neighbor, not even music-hating aliens from *outer fucking space*, was going to stop her from rocking it. Nobody ever had, nobody ever would.

Now if only she could find a way to convince the harp to let her hook it up to a distortion pedal.

# A NICE SHORT CONVERSATION

## ROBERT J. MCCARTER

*Robert J. McCarter gives us with this story a science fiction story (well sort of) full of very real human life.*

*Robert has published at least seven novels, and his short fiction has appeared or is forthcoming in* The Saturday Evening Post, Fiction River, Andromeda Spaceways Inflight Magazine, *and numerous anthologies. Plus, he sells me stories here regularly.*

*Look for more of Robert's work at his web site https:// robertjmccarter.com/*

# A NICE SHORT CONVERSATION

## ROBERT J. MCCARTER

L et me tell you a story. Not quite "once upon a time" but something along those lines.

This story takes place in our remote galaxy in our dainty little solar system in the middle of a large continent in the northern hemisphere in a tiny bedroom in a small house. There, an amorphous blue ball of energy—which we will refer to as "Al"—was floating in a darkened bedroom above a bed which contained the trashing from of a four-year-old girl named Bee.

Even though a human designation such as "Al" is not appropriate here, considering the whole "amorphous blue ball of energy" thing, a little anthropomorphizing will help, so let's just go with it. On the other hand, "Bee" is entirely an appropriate designation for the little girl, for that was her name.

In this particular bedroom, the bed was made up with a puffy comforter in purple and pink with a pattern of bears. Under that comforter, Bee was tossing and turning and moaning in her sleep.

The lacy curtains in this tiny room were open, letting silver moonlight splash in and giving everything a ghostly hue. It was a warm evening, so the window was open a bit, and the curtains undulated gracefully in the breeze.

Bee is easy enough to understand, little girls having nightmares are quite common, so let's turn our attention to Al as they hovered above Bee, their amorphous blue form pulsing in curiosity. It must be noted that Al was a being of pure energy, an ancient being and it was quite surprising that they were in this bedroom curious about this girl.

And, yes, if you are wondering, they/them above is used in reference to Al because the words are gender-neutral. Al is not biological and therefore does not have a biological gender. And it doesn't hurt that they/them also hint that Al doesn't have the sense of individuality that you or I have.

So, Al, the aforementioned amorphous blue ball of energy, floated above Bee, and they were as worried as a being of pure energy could be. About Bee. Al had felt something and traveled a very long way to investigate it. They hadn't felt something like this in a very long time.

And Al wasn't worried at Bee's tossing and turning, at her gentle moaning, at her grasping hands and tangle of dark brown hair. These were all too biological for Al to worry about. They were worried at what they felt, because that moaning and tossing and turning came from a deep place, from a place that Al did understand and care for.

Al was not just worried, but confused. They had traveled far at considerable expense to themselves, and instead of their fond hopes being realized and finding a being like themselves, they found this little biological girl in the throes of a nightmare.

Which is what we must explore next.

————

That night before Bee went to bed, her parents had been fighting. Drinking and fighting. Enough for her father to yell at her mother and say dark and terrible things Bee didn't understand completely. Enough for her mother to scream at her father and throw things at him and demand that he leave.

Like most children, Bee had thought that it was her fault. That the vase she had bumped into earlier, that had shattered on the tile floor of the hallway with such a sharp sound, that she had cut herself trying to clean up before anyone saw, and that her crying over it all had started the fight.

Children believe the world revolves around them, and, on a certain level, it does. Bee was a busy and active girl and required a lot of attention.

After her father had stormed out and her mother had drunk more and they were sitting in the living room with a cartoon playing on the TV, she had asked, "Are you and Daddy getting a divorce?" Bee had a bit of a lisp so it sounded more like "divorth" and would under other circumstances be considered entirely adorable.

Her mother blanched and coughed on the red wine she had been drinking. When she could reply, she said, "I don't know."

Bee's mother did not believe in lying to her child. Not that she didn't ever lie, she just tried not to and with all the alcohol she had on board altering her biology, the truth slipped out before she could think of how it would affect her child.

Bee was a sensitive little girl, and while she didn't quite understand what divorce meant—she thought maybe it meant she would never see either of her parents again—she was terrified by the prospect and started crying immediately.

This was not the tentative cry of a child that had scraped its knee and hadn't felt the full impact of the pain and was just starting to wind up to a good cry just in case. This was pain and fear that Bee felt deeply, and the amount of the tears and volume of the crying matched.

It took her mother a good hour to calm her and then another hour to get her to sleep.

This was why Bee was tossing in her bed while Al was hovering above her.

———

Before all of this, Al, the amorphous blue ball of energy, had been minding their own business out past the Kuiper Belt hanging out and doing what conscious blobs of energy usually do.

And I guess that's a pretty worthless stab at explaining the life of a very alien life form. Let me try again.

Al had been out in the darkness of space *feeling*.

Again, not very useful but a lot closer.

Al had been wandering through this part of our fine little galaxy trying to find a kindred…hmmm, dare I say, soul.

It had been millennia since Al had found a kindred spirit, a being similar enough to themselves that they could have a nice conversation. And I know that sounds like a long time, and it was, but for Al it was a drop in the very large bucket of a very long life, but it had been long enough that they had become lonely.

Al had flitted from star to star and planet to planet and had, indeed, found some interesting energy emanations, but solar flares didn't talk back, and nebulae were horrible conversationalists. Al was well equipped to amuse themselves, but even at that, a kind of loneliness had set in.

When Al first cruised through our dainty little solar system in our remote galaxy, they noticed the beings on the third rock from the sun. At that point, fire was the big innovation and while language was coming, there was a lot of grunting involved, but still Al found something intriguing in the tight ball of electrical energy contained in the roundish housing of bone that rode atop these bipedal creatures.

They were curious if anything interesting would become of it, even though biological life wasn't really their cup of tea, so messy and all. Nevertheless, they remembered our dainty little solar system and the planet in the perfect position to support biological life and added it to their list of things to watch and moved on.

Al came back when bronze was the thing, and then iron, and then steel, and finally silicon and the crazy things you could do with it and electricity. They delighted over the development of so many languages and did their best to listen in on the radio waves emanating from the planet, but it all became too much and too confusing.

So many voices each trying to be louder than the other. So many wars and injustices. On this visit to our out-of-the-way galaxy and our dainty solar system, they got no closer than the Kuiper Belt, finding the electromagnetic chaos to be just too much, until they felt Bee tossing and turning under her purple-and-pink comforter. Until they felt what might just be what they were looking for. But how could that be? Was there one out of the billions of beings on this planet of chaos that they just might be able to have a nice conversation with?

Al had no choice, but rushed to the little girl in distress.

————

So now this all must make sense. A little girl afraid of abandonment tossing and turning in her sleep and an amorphous blue ball of energy many millennia old wondering if this biological being could be what they were looking for.

At the start, I told you that Al was as worried as they could be, and you might be wondering why. Well, that's pretty simple. Even Al has their biases, and in their great explorations they hadn't been that impressed with biology. It wasn't just biological beings' extremely fleeting existence, but their seemingly universal insistence on an insane level of individuality that regularly led them to do terrible things to each other.

So, Al feared that Bee was not what they were looking for, and then they feared that if she was, it would be the shortest conversation of their very long life and they would be alone in the universe again trying to find someone to talk to.

But one does not survive for millennia and travel the universe and not know courage.

And while Al didn't understand this, it must be said that a four-year-old girl fearing that both of her parents are about to abandon her knows quite a bit about fear and courage too.

So, floating above the distressed child, Al did their best to ignore all that messy biology and focus on the ball of electromagnetic energy contained in the roundish housing of bone that belonged to the biological being Bee. It was never easy to get through to biological beings in ways that did not shatter their fragile sense of individuality, but Al had done it several times over the many millennia, and this particular entity was a young one, so they knew that while success was not assured it was in the realm of possibilities.

This brings us to the rather fraught question of how does an amorphous blob of blue energy communicate with a troubled little girl? Well, if you were in that room with the curtains open and the ghostly glow of the moon throwing a silver light on the pink-and-purple comforter and you had eyes that could see Al, you would have seen tiny tendrils of blue snake out from the amorphous blue blob floating in the air and tentatively connecting with the child's head.

When this happened, Bee stopped her tossing and turning and lay there still on her back, her breath evening and her heart slowing.

Al was as careful as they could be and used all of their time in our remote galaxy and our dainty little solar system and all that they had learned about messy biology to not hurt this being, to find a way to reach Bee.

This was not easy. It was harder than flitting from star to star. Harder than traveling from the Kuiper Belt to this planet. Harder than anything they had done in a very long time.

They were a "they" and she was an "I" and it was a distinction so basic that it was a very far distance to bridge.

The amorphous ball of blue energy that was Al pulsed and shrunk in ways that appeared to be painful, but still Al persisted.

For Al it was one of the fastest and most deliberate things they had ever done, for Bee, it was over three hours of lying still, feeling such things as she had never felt before. At first scary but then strangely comforting.

At the end of this time, Al was floating right above Bee's head, an uncountable number of tiny tendrils extending from them into the little girl's head, the blue ball of amorphous energy that was them no longer pulsing or chaotic but a pure and peaceful blue, a rather happy blue, it must be said.

It was then that Bee's eyes flicked open. "Who are you?" she asked, a smile lighting up her round face.

———————

B ee was at the kitchen table playing with Play-Doh when her mother finally came downstairs. This was not a good morning for Bee's mother, a stabbing pain in her head and her eyes red-rimmed from crying and a lack of restful sleep.

She stood there hugging her worn brown robe around her, staring at her daughter, who was humming and rolling a blue piece of Play-Doh and then holding it in the air above her head, her hand moving it gently back and forth like it was hovering there.

Bee's mother could not hear her daughter clearly, but she appeared to be having a happy conversation, the kind she hadn't heard her daughter have in quite some time.

"Good morning, honey," she said. "You seem to be feeling better."

"Yes," Bee said in a clipped, distracted way.

Bee's mother went over and got a cup of coffee, grateful that she had remembered to set it up the night before. She leaned against the Formica counter of their small kitchen and stared at her daughter. She blew on her coffee and had a sip while Bee continued to have an animated conversation she couldn't quite hear.

She was worried. She knew her daughter, and while Bee got over the little things quickly, what happened last night was not a little thing at all.

"What game are you playing?" she asked.

Bee looked up and smiled, the girl's brown eyes wide and clear. "I'm pretending I'm Al," she said with a smile.

Bee's mother racked her hungover brain and couldn't think of an Al that Bee would know. "Who is Al?" she asked.

Bee smiled. "My new friend. He came from the stars." Of course, Bee's adorable lisp was in play so she said, "He came from the tharth."

Bee's mother sipped her coffee and tried to wake up. So her daughter had an imaginary friend that wasn't a faerie but an alien. That wasn't that far off for her creative girl.

"Al told me Daddy will be back tonight," Bee said with a smile. "And Al said that he likes talking to me so I will never be alone even if you and Daddy get a divorth."

Bee's mother stared at her daughter. It was a call from Bee's father that had woken her up. They still had things to work through, but they had both been stupid last night...and drunk. He was planning to come home after work.

Bee's mother convinced herself that Bee must have overheard the conversation and was happy that her daughter was feeling better.

———

Al was true to their word and stayed with Bee for the brief flickering of her biological life. Bee soon learned to stop telling people about her "imaginary" friend, who she knew to be quite real, and enjoyed the companionship.

Al and Bee were together as Bee grew from a girl into a teenager. As Bee navigated the confusing pathways of adolescence, her journey through it calmer than most because she never felt like she was alone, her sense of self was not as strong as her peers. There was always Al, and while Al felt like a part of her, she knew that they were not.

Al and Bee were together when Bee met the man that would be her husband, when she had her first child, when she witnessed the birth of her first grandchild, and when, finally, she was old and dying.

It was in a similar room that Al had first seen four-year-old Bee that the ninety-four-year-old Bee died. It was a small room with gauzy white curtains and a purple comforter—though gone were the bear prints—with the silver glow of the moon washing in.

Bee's son was asleep in an old recliner and, if you had eyes to see it, Al was there hovering above the withered gray-haired woman, the many thin blue tendrils reaching from their amorphous blue form into the roundish housing of bone that contained the electromagnetic emanations that Al had been having a nice short conversation with.

The conversation, for the most part, had stopped, but Al wasn't sad. All things have beginnings, and all things have endings, and they knew that. But they would miss this nice short conversation with this lovely biological being.

And while it was short, Al had learned much about biological beings and found that their prejudices about biology and individuality, while founded in truth, had not been the whole truth. In their time with Bee, they had had seen acts of courage and compassion that gave them hope for biological beings.

For her part, Bee was content with her time on this planet. She had never felt like she was alone, and her life slipped away without drama or struggle.

And if you had the eyes to see it and were watching, you would have seen a small amorphous ball of blue energy emerge from the roundish housing of bone that contained the fading embers of Bee's electromagnetic energies that Al had so enjoyed communicating with.

As Al's tendrils withdrew, this new bit of amorphous blue joined the larger amorphous blue ball. Al hovered there for a while over the abandoned biological form, taking a moment to integrate this new bit of energy before zooming out the window into the silvery moonlight.

Al, now with that little bit of Bee, resumed their quest to find someone to have a nice conversation with out among the stars.

# THE BOBS
## ANNIE REED

Professional writer Annie Reed writes stories that span genres and are always powerful. In fact, with Annie, you just never know the type of story you might be reading, but you will always know it will grab you and be a compelling read.

So far Annie has had a story in every issue of the magazine and in a lot of these fun extra volumes, and as the editor, I hope to continue that streak. You will understand why after you read this story that made me really uncomfortable, but as Annie's main character says, "I am one of those people."

Annie's stories have appeared in four best mystery stories of the year volumes so far. Look for so much more of Annie's work at her website https://anniereed.wordpress.com/

# THE BOBS

## ANNIE REED

My mother is one of *those* people.

You know the type. Fifteen years ago she couldn't program the correct time on her VCR to save her soul, much less record her favorite soap opera. Ten years ago she didn't understand the remote for her DVD player. A few years after that when she mused about the possibility of buying an XBox360 for my newly retired father, who was starting to spend far too much time with his fishing buddies drinking beer instead of catching fish, I had visions of late-night phone calls asking if I knew how to make the remote controller work. Just because I happen to be my parents' late-in-life daughter doesn't mean I'm a video game wiz. I hurried to point out that if she bought him a video game, he'd be home all the time playing video games instead of out with his buddies. She got him a new fishing hat instead.

So imagine my surprise when I stopped by my mother's house last weekend and she showed me her new tablet. No,

97

not an iPad, but a rather good imitation. I didn't recognize the brand.

"Uh," I said, temporarily at a loss for words. I don't have a tablet. I can barely afford my smartphone.

We were sitting at my parents' kitchen table. Unlike the cluttered table in my own apartment that seems to magnetically attract all manner of un-kitchen-like things—including my latest knitting project, the stack of pre-street DVDs I was supposed to watch (yes, I work in one of the world's last surviving video stores), and a stack of unread cooking, bridal, and parenting magazines I don't remember subscribing to (I think my mother secretly signed me up for these things hoping I'll catch the hint; subtle, she's not)—my mother's table was strictly kitchen appropriate, complete with plastic tablecloth and a napkin holder in the exact center.

Mom had a cup of tea—Lady Grey, decaf—brewed in a teapot she bought from one of those shopping channel shows. I was on my second cup of coffee.

My mother makes kickass coffee. She's tried to teach me how, but my coffee-making skills are nonexistent. So are my cooking skills, hence the state of my kitchen table. Most of my meals are fast food, and I eat them in the living room.

My mom's new tablet was sleek and glossy black with just a few recessed, unlabeled buttons. I wouldn't have a clue what to do when my mother started in with the inevitable *I don't understand how you*…questions.

"It's nice," I finally said.

"Isn't it just?" My mother took the tablet from me like she was handling a newborn. I was happy enough to hand it over. Those things cost more than I make in half a month, and the last thing I wanted to do was drop hers. "You'd be amazed at what it does."

Well, that was surprising. And here I thought I'd have my hands full trying to figure out my mom's new tech.

"You're not having any troubles with it?" I asked.

She raised an eyebrow at me. My mother has the uncanny ability, much like Mr. Spock in the original *Star Trek*, to say volumes with one raised eyebrow. "I'm not an idiot, Jane."

"Of course, you're not," I said. "It's just..." I waved a hand in the general direction of my parents' living room where, for years, the VCR had sat blinking its little display, waiting in vain for someone to set the clock.

She smiled down at the tablet. "Bob is user-friendly," she said.

Bob? "You named your tablet?"

"It tells you to in the instructions," she said.

I blinked. "You read the instructions?"

Was this really my mother? Maybe I should look for the pod to make sure she hadn't been body snatched by evil aliens.

"Well, there weren't many instructions," she said. "All I had to do was turn it on, and the screen told me exactly what to do. Even your father could have managed it."

That was my mother's shorthand for *even an idiot could have figured it out*. My father is to all things automotive as my mother is to all things electronic. He's been known to turn a simple oil change he tried to do himself into the need for a major engine overhaul.

"Would you like to see?" she asked. "Bob likes to show off."

Bob again. It was like I suddenly had a new sibling. "Sure."

I watched as my mother pressed one of the unlabeled buttons on the top of the tablet then slid her finger across the shiny black surface. The screen winked on, but instead of a field full of application icons, a man's face filled the frame.

"Good morning, Roberta," the tablet said.

It talked to her. Neat trick. No wonder my mother liked the thing.

"Good morning, Bob," my mother said. "This is my daughter. You remember I told you about Jane?" She turned the tablet so that it faced me. "Say good morning, Jane."

Feeling more than a little like an idiot, I said, "Good morning, Bob," and did a finger wave.

"Good morning, Jane," the tablet said, and the face on the screen smiled at me. "It's nice to finally meet you. Your mother has told me a lot about you."

I nearly dropped my coffee cup. Not only was the tablet—Bob—talking to me, but the face on the screen didn't have that simulated person, video-game look. It was like I was talking to a real person on the other end of a video conference call, only without the jerky, please-wait-while-we-buffer look.

"She has?" I managed to squeak out. I looked at my mother. She was beaming at Bob like a proud parent.

"Only good things," my mother said. She tilted the tablet so we both could see it. "Bob, can you show me my schedule for this next week?"

"Of course."

The face on the screen turned to the left. A small window opened, displaying a calendar for the week. My mother's book club meeting was prominently displayed along with a little open book symbol.

"I think I need an appointment to get my hair cut and

permed." My mother wore her light gray hair short and in a style I call Dandelion Fluff. "Can you take care of that for me?"

For a moment, I thought she was asking me to call her hairdresser, then I realized she was speaking to the tablet.

"Of course," Bob said.

The tablet emitted what seemed like random sounds as the screen dimmed, then I realized it was playing the tune from *Final Jeopardy*.

"It can do that?" I asked. "Make your appointments for you?"

"Of course," my mother said. "Just watch."

Sure enough, less than a minute later, the image of the handsome man was back on screen. "Appointment scheduled," Bob said. "Tuesday at ten thirty a.m."

How in the world?

And how did my mother figure it out?

"You learned how to do all that just by reading the instructions on the screen?" I asked.

"Well..." My mother put the tablet on the table gently. "Bob walked me through most of it. He's a marvelous feature, don't you think? And smart, too. I only have to tell him things once and he does them. Imagine that."

Unlike my father. His ability to tune my mother out is, I'm sure, directly responsible for their forty-one years of marriage.

That explained my father. Nothing I knew of explained Bob. I mean, sure, I supposed the tablet could interface with a computer at my mother's beauty salon, but the last time I'd gone with her when she got her hair done, there hadn't even been a computerized cash register in the place, much less a computerized scheduling system.

"Do you still have the box Bob came in?" I asked.

My mother gave me the eyebrow again.

"I just want to see where you got it, in case I want to get a Bob of my own."

I was pretty sure she didn't believe me, but she brought the box out from the bedroom my parents use as an office/library/keep-all-the-stuff-we-don't-want-company-to-see room. Everything, include the static-free cover the tablet had been encased in on arrival, was still inside the box.

I opened the little booklet of instructions, flipped past the page that identified all the unnamed buttons on the tablet, and found the "Let's Get Started!" section.

It was half a page long. As my mother had said, the only instruction was to press the button she'd pressed, slide a finger across the screen, and follow the instructions of the on-screen genie.

Huh.

Genie. Not wizard.

Bob's face was still on the tablet's screen. He wore a contented expression, like a man born to wait. I squinted my eyes and tried to imagine him bare-chested and with a turban on his head. Yes, I've watched too many Disney movies in my life, why do you ask? Still, even with a good mental image of the cartoon genie from *Aladdin* wedged firmly in my brain, I couldn't see the resemblance to Bob. For one thing, Bob wasn't blue. He was dark-haired and dark-eyed, but he was square-jawed and rather bland-looking, even if he was bland-looking in a handsome way. Sort of like Jake Gyllenhaal in *Prince of Persia*. Only older. Maybe. With Bob it was hard to tell.

I turned the instruction booklet over and studied the name

of the tablet company on the back. Not one I recognized, but I wasn't surprised. I tried to make a note of the name in the part of my brain that actually remembers the things I'm supposed to remember, and handed the booklet back to my mother.

"Very cool," I said. "I'll have to look into it."

My mother seemed pleased with herself. I wasn't exactly sure why, but her smile made me nervous.

———

Three days later, I answered my door to find a Federal Express delivery man waiting for me.

"Sign here," he said, thrusting an electronic reader at my face.

"Who's this for?" I asked. I hadn't ordered anything recently, much less anything that Federal Express would need a signature for.

The delivery man read my name off the box he had tucked beneath his arm. "That's you, right?"

"Yeah, but I…" Then I noticed the name on the box. The company that made my mother's tablet. I tried not to groan. "Yeah, that's me."

Now I know why my mother had smiled like that.

She'd bought her poor, single, underemployed daughter a Bob of her own.

I could almost understand her reasoning. Her Bob had turned out to be a wonderful companion. I lived alone. I hadn't had a boyfriend in years, didn't seem at all interested in giving her grandchildren even with all the magazine subscriptions she'd bought me, and I didn't even have a cat for company. She was just doing something nice. I wasn't quite sure how she could afford to buy me a tablet—Dad was retired, after all, and Mom had never worked outside the home—but she'd be hurt if I didn't accept it.

I signed the Fed Ex guy's electronic reader and accepted my package of Bob.

Instead of opening the package right away, I plopped it on the kitchen table next to the towering stack of unread magazines. I really should throw the things out, but part of me is convinced my mother will know if I throw the magazines away unread, so they just accumulate. It's not like I need my kitchen table for eating, right?

I took the top DVD off my stack of pre-street copies. Staff were encouraged—and by that, I mean in a *do it or you're fired* kind of way—to watch every new movie during the week before it went on the floor for rent. In theory, that meant store employees could suggest something to customers who asked for recommendations. In reality, that meant not only did I spend eight hours a day, five days a week surrounded by more movies than a person could watch in a lifetime, I also spent at least ten hours of my evenings and days off watching movies. No wonder I didn't date. The minute any guy suggested taking me out to a movie, my eyes crossed and I heard our company's stupid little jingle from the trailer DVD that played nonstop from the time my store opened until we closed up shop for the night.

I was halfway through the latest independent film, a dialogue-heavy, plot-thin family drama, when I heard a suspicious beeping coming from my kitchen.

I muted the sound on my television. No, it wasn't the quiet beep from my dishwasher telling me it was time to put the clean dishes away. It wasn't the timer on my stove, not that I ever used the stove, and it wasn't the shrill screech of the smoke detector. This was an insistent beep that I felt inside my head as much as heard.

Weird.

I couldn't ignore the sound, much as I would have liked to take the nap the independent flick was encouraging me to take, so I got up and went into the kitchen. There I found the package full of my very own Bob beeping away like crazy.

"Well, aren't you insistent?" I said.

Might as well get this over with. I opened the package and unwrapped the tablet. I half expected to see Bob's face on the screen, but the only thing on the display was an arrow that pointed to the On button. Written on the arrow was "Press Here."

I pressed there.

Another arrow appeared instructing me to slide my finger across the screen, so I did, and Bob appeared. Only it wasn't quite the same Bob of my mother's tablet. My Bob had sandy-brown hair, green eyes, and not quite as square a jaw. He was still handsome, though, for a tablet genie.

"Good afternoon," my Bob said.

"Hello," I said back. "My name is—"

"Jane. Pleased to meet you, Jane."

I did the eyebrow raise. How did it know my name? "How come you know who I am?"

"Your name was on the delivery slip," Bob said. "You are Jane, aren't you?"

The delivery slip. Of course. I should have known that the tablet—the *tablet*, for goodness sake—would know what was written on the delivery slip.

"I've got a sneaking suspicion about you," I told Bob. "Want to hear it?"

Now, I've watched more movies than I can remember. I've always liked movies (or I used to), which is why I went to work in a video store in the first place. That and they were hiring, and it was either video store rental clerk or waitress in a skimpy uniform, and movies won out.

I've read a lot of books, too, and I've always had an open mind about things. Sure, I suppose tablets like Bob might be explained away as the next level in artificial intelligence, but I doubted people like my mother could afford that kind of technology once, let alone twice. I'd done a little internet browsing for the company that manufactured the Bob tablets, and I'd found nothing. Well, almost nothing. It seemed the company advertised in one place and one place only—*Modern Housekeeping* magazine. The only how-to-be-a-good-homemaker magazine my mother hadn't subscribed me to.

"Would you like to set me up now?" Bob asked.

"I'm not that easily distracted," I said. "And I'm not sixty-seven years old."

I could almost hear Bob sigh before his features settled into the same man-content-to-wait expression I'd seen on my mother's Bob.

"You're a genie," I said.

Now Bob did the eyebrow raise. "That's it? Of course, I'm a genie. That's what my system calls me. Computers have wizards to walk their users through programs. Our tablets have genies. Hence, I'm a genie."

I must have hit a nerve. Bob had gone verbose.

"No, a genie. As in, alakazam, puff-of-smoke genie. As in grant me three—"

I stopped myself as the idea really hit me. Holy crap! What if the Bobs really were genies? Did that mean my mother got three wishes? That could be dangerous. I mean, I could find myself married with children and *liking* it!

Except she'd had her tablet long enough to make three wishes already, hadn't she? I'd sat right there while she'd asked Bob to make her an appointment for a haircut. If she'd made her three wishes and Bob the genie left her tablet, she would have called me asking me for help to fix it. Wouldn't she?

"You have to say the word," the Bob on my tablet said.

"What word?"

Now both his eyebrows went up, and his expression was far from content.

"Ah," I said. "The W word."

"Yes."

Bob was talking to me, but I got it. My mother hadn't said the W word. In fact, I didn't think my mother had ever said the W word in her life. She was a practical, if tech-deficient, woman.

"I think you better tell me the rules," I said to my Bob.

"That's outside my programming."

"Even if I use the W word?"

"You only get three. Use them wisely."

Well, I'd need to know the rules if I was going to play along, and it looked like I was. "I wish you'd tell me what's going on here so I know what my mother's gotten me into," I said.

Bob nodded at me. "Your wish is my command."

I've been around techy things all my life. I guess it comes with being born into a generation that had VCRs and microwaves and marveled that cell phones used to be just science fiction. I've pored over instruction manuals for printers and copiers and fax machines and scanners. I've called tech support for credit card machines and computers and the security system at our store. I've browsed through shelf after shelf of books on how to use computer software. So I suppose I was expecting Bob to rattle off hour after hour of increasingly complex explanations about how genies ended up in tablets.

Not so much. What he did say only took him about a minute.

"We upgraded," he said. "Nobody buys magic lamps anymore, and even if they did, you ever try to get someone to rub one? Everything's technology these days. People have more gadgets with more apps that do more things than any one person can do in a lifetime. But the rules are the same. Every person who rubs a finger across the screen—"

Like my mother and I both did, just like the instructions told us to.

"—wakes up the genie inside. We can grant our owner three wishes, and then we're set free."

"What happens to the tablet after you're gone?"

"Second wish?" Bob asked.

I shook my head. "Part of the first wish. You didn't tell me all the rules." I'd have to remember that the Bobs were tricky.

"The tablet performs like any other tablet."

In other words, it wouldn't make my mother's appointments for her. Keep track of them, yes, just like any other tablet, but she'd have to make the call herself and type the information into the app.

"You have two more wishes left," Bob said.

I wouldn't mind having a tablet that was just a tablet, just like I didn't mind having a job at the video store. Provided that mail-order DVDs and online video streaming didn't put us out of business, that is. But my mother seemed really happy with her Bob. She'd be miserable if he left.

"Okay," I said. "I've got it." I told Bob the name of my company's primary competitor.

"I've got an app for that," Bob said.

"I don't doubt it. I wish they'd do something really stupid so they don't put all the video stores out of business."

Bob smiled at me. "Any specifics?"

I smiled back. "Use your imagination," I said.

"Your wish is my command."

Bob winked off the screen for so long that I thought I'd broken him. I was about to go unpause my dialogue-heavy indie pre-street when Bob's face reappeared on my screen.

"Done," he said. "It might take a little time, but done. Are you ready for your third wish?"

I was. I'd thought about it while Bob was gone, and it seemed like the right thing to do. "I wish," I said, eyeing Bob probably for the last time, "that my mother forgets the word 'wish.'"

The oddest expression came over his face, part surprise, part curiosity, and part gentle understanding.

"Done," he said, and winked out of existence, leaving behind a screen full of icons.

And a low battery warning.

After all that work? No kidding.

---

My mother still has her Bob. He makes her hair appointments and reminds her of her book club meetings. I think he orders magazine subscriptions for me, too, given that I'm now subscribed to magazines on history, mythology, psychology, and, just for good measure, elder care.

I got the message. Thanks to me, her Bob will never be able to leave the tablet, at least not while my mother's so attached to it, and he's a little miffed.

But I know something Bob doesn't know. My mother is the queen of gadgets. She's always been intrigued by the next new thing. If the gadget's electronic, she may not understand how to use it, but that doesn't stop her from getting it if the mood strikes her.

Bob will eventually be replaced by something new that catches her attention, and he'll find himself alone and forgotten in a drawer in that room my parents use to keep things they don't want company to see.

Like the little electronic dictionary with the tiny keyboard my mother bought when she and my father were both doing crossword puzzles and playing Scrabble.

Or the handheld mixer my mother bought because she'd seen on TV how it whipped non-fat milk just like whipped cream. Only when she tried it, she discovered whipped non-fat milk still tasted like non-fat milk, and my father refused to have any of it on his pumpkin pie.

After the new has worn off and my mother moves on to the next thing, I'll retrieve her Bob from the drawer where she left him. I'll turn him on and make three wishes and let him go. I figure if he's been in a lamp waiting hundreds of years for someone to come by and rub the thing, he can wait for a few months or even a few years until my mother tires of her tablet.

Until then, he's going to get to know my mother's hairdresser real well, and I might find myself subscribed to some really interesting reading material.

I just hope my mailman doesn't hate me. He's actually kind of cute.

# WALKING THE DOG

## J. STEVEN YORK

*J. Steven York is a master at writing some of the most twisted and fun stories being published. And this original one hits the voice perfectly of twisted and fun. And head-shaking.*

*Steve has been publishing novels and powerful short fiction for over thirty years now, and before that he worked writing in the gaming industry. Steve is also doing a really fun and off-the-wall internet comic, one of which he has allowed me to put in each issue on the back page.*

WALKING THE DOG
by Steven York

# WALKING THE DOG

## J. STEVEN YORK

"Drink me," said the alien in the toilet.

"Drink me," it said.

Meanwhile, in the living room, Myrtle the dog lay on her cedar-scented dog bed in front of the fireplace, dreaming of rolling, summer-green hills and chasing rabbits.

"Drink me," said the alien, its voice echoing in the ceramic bowl.

It was a creature of complex molecules suspended in water, a liquid lifeform. As a cloud of vapor floating through interstellar space, it had traveled a thousand Earth years, and a dozen light years, following deduction, reasoning, and, at the last, radio signals, in order to find that toilet.

"Drink me," it called.

It had plunged through the atmosphere as a cloud of steam, and rained into the planet's largest ocean. It had wandered for years, decades, until it had realized that the intelligent, technological creatures of this world lived on *land*. So the alien had journeyed up rivers, streams, and finally

115

through tanks and pipes, into the home of one of the intelligences it had come so far to join with.

"Drink me," said the alien.

In the living room, Myrtle's ears twitched. She lifted her head to look around the room. "Woof," said Myrtle.

"Drink me," the small voice echoed from down the hall.

"Woof," said Myrtle, climbing to her feet after a small hesitation. She padded over to the window, nosed past the closed drapes, and looked out at the empty sidewalk. "Woof-woof," she said as a precautionary measure.

But nothing moved. No people. No rabbits. The yard was empty. The walk was empty. The street was empty. "Woof."

"Drink me," said the voice.

Myrtle pulled her head out of the window and padded into the hall, nails clicking on the hardwood floor.

"Drink me!"

The voice came through the bedroom, but Myrtle didn't recognize the voice, and she knew her people weren't home. She lowered her head and sniffed the floor. Only her people, house dust, Lemon Pledge, and her own personal odor. She started down the hall to investigate further when she spotted her ball. It was a tennis ball, once fuzzy fluorescent yellow, now threadbare off-brown, still damp with drool.

She grabbed the ball, tilting her head back and chewing joyfully.

"Drink me," said the voice.

Myrtle tried to woof, but with the ball in her mouth it came out more like "Arruoo." She dropped the ball on the carpet just inside the bedroom door and immediately forgot about it. She sniffed the unmade bed, always a comforting source of people smells, or at least interesting laundry chemicals. Nothing strange.

"Drink me," the voice echoed from the bathroom.

"Woof," said Myrtle. "Woof."

She walked cautiously into the bathroom, the tile floor cool under the pads of her feet. She looked around expectantly, but saw no one. She nosed aside the clammy shower curtain. It smelled of soap, sweat, shampoo, wet hair and faintly of mildew.

Empty.

"Drink me."

She turned to stare at the toilet, intent on the sound of the voice.

"Drink me," it said. "Drink me."

Unfortunately, while Myrtle had a considerable English vocabulary, including "come," "sit," "heel," and "No, dammit," it included neither "drink" nor "me."

Fortunately, while she didn't understand much about English, Myrtle *did* understand about toilet bowls. Unable to find the invader, she surrendered to the call of the leaky float valve. Cool, fresh water hissed into the bowl. She dipped her muzzle into the toilet. There was an unfamiliar sweet smell, but it was pleasant enough. She hesitated only a moment, and began to lap.

The alien said nothing, at least in English, or words, or sounds, but it sent a chemical signal that would have been interpreted by another of its kind as "Wheeeee!"

Even before it had reached Myrtle's stomach the alien became one with the fluids of her body, sensing the coursing of water through every vein, artery, membrane, and cell of her body.

The alien was overwhelmed, both with the mechanical crudity of the body, and the complexity of its processes. Unable to analyze it all at once, the alien focused on the rapid, dynamic, complex systems that must control the intelligence.

Myrtle lifted her head and blinked. The water tasted strange, but something else was happening.

"Take me to your leader," said the voice in her head.

That was strange.

"Take me to your leader!"

The voice spoke, and she *understood. The voice wanted to find her people!*

Good idea!

Excited at the realization, she trotted from room to room, looking for them, finding their smell in the laundry hamper, and under the kitchen table, and in the recliner, and in the office chair.

But her people weren't there. In the excitement of understanding, she'd forgotten. She looked hopefully out the office window, but the driveway was still empty. Her people weren't there. The excitement and urgency faded. She sat down and scratched at a flea behind her left ear.

By then, the alien knew something was wrong. As complex as this creature was, it was not the life form that had sent those radio signals. It seemed unlikely the creature had much technology at all. But it lived with those that did. It moved among them. It would do, for the alien's purposes. It would get the alien where it needed to go.

Feeling its way through her brain, it modified the flow of molecules through certain cell walls, altered the flow of electrons from cell to cell.

Myrtle blinked. *Voices.* Somehow, she needed to hear

people. She stared at the blank eye of the television with a comprehension she'd never had before. She remembered people touching the box, making it loud and bright.

In the past, the box had been annoying, not interesting. Her people paid attention to the box, and not to her. But now it somehow seemed *important. She* needed to make it loud and bright!

Myrtle bumped her nose against the box. It left a wet smudge on the cold surface.

Nothing.

She scratched at it with her front paw. One her claws caught on a rough spot. The box clicked and squealed, another reason she didn't like it. But it became bright, and the voices came.

Myrtle sat, transfixed, noticing for the first time that the moving lights were *pictures.* It was like a poor version of seeing a thing, but now she understood. For an hour she watched, soap operas and talk shows and commercials. She'd never known the box was so wonderful. Then a woman came on the box. She looked out of the box and said, "The President of the United States will shortly address a gathering of high school students at Kent Patterson Park." The words still meant nothing to Myrtle, but she felt something within her stir in response to them. She studied the pictures that splashed on the screen, of restless people sitting in rows of chairs, And a large machine settling out of the sky onto a grassy hilltop, disgorging a smiling, waving man and a crowd of other people.

Something inside Myrtle wanted to go to this place and see this man. She jumped with the excitement of it. She *knew* where he was. Her people took her to that park to play and walk. She could get there. But only if she could get out of the house.

She ran to the front door. *Closed.* She ran to the back door. *Closed.* She whined in frustration and scratched at the door. Then she looked at the knob. She'd always known it had *something* to do with opening the door. But now it seemed so much clearer. She took the knob in her mouth. It was hard and cold, and the metal tasted funny. But she bit down and turned. The metal slipped against her teeth, and it hurt, but she tried again. The knob turned. The door clicked. Myrtle released the knob and dropped to the floor.

The door slowly swung open, and a rainbow of outside smells wafted in. Myrtle whined and ran in circles. *This was great.*

She trotted down the driveway and down the street, past rows of houses, and sweet, soft lawns. Occasionally, she would be distracted by a smell, or a sound, or a child on a bicycle, or a foraging squirrel, but each time the strange feeling inside her pulled her back on track.

She walked for blocks. Past bakeries, school yards and gas stations, crossing busy streets and dodging traffic. The last few blocks cars and people seemed to be everywhere, making it difficult for Myrtle to recognize landmarks. She backtracked several times, sniffing and circling to get her bearings.

Finally, she found the playground at the edge of the park. It was empty except for strange restless men in dark clothes. None of them were playing, and none of them seemed playful. She kept her distance and none of them seemed to notice her.

She followed a trail through a patch of woods and up a hillside to where the big machine squatted silently. There were more of the dark men pacing around the big machine, but the smiling man was gone. One of the dark men saw her, and yelled. He chased her for a few steps and waved his arms as she easily trotted away from him. Down the other side of the hill she could see the rows of chairs filled with people, all watching a man who spoke in the loudest voice she'd ever heard. It was the smiling man.

Her tail beat the air furiously. She was so happy to see him, it was almost like he was one of her *people*. She trotted down the hill, steering wide of the dark men who surrounded the platform where the smiling man stood.

She crouched in a clump of bushes, tail beating the ground behind her. Only a few hundred feet of open space separated her from the stairs to the platform. The feeling inside her urged her on. She could see the smiling man, and she wondered what he smelled like. Then, from somewhere inside her, another, more familiar, urge. She ignored it.

She trotted across the grass, slowing to a fast walk as she crossed a closed off street. As she crossed the far curb, a dog smell jerked her off the path. She followed it up the gutter, and over to a metal object surrounded by dozens of dog smells. The smiling man was forgotten as she sniffed around the fire hydrant. The feeling inside her tried to call her away, but this was more important. She backed up to the hydrant and squatted.

The alien wailed as it parted company with Myrtle. It had come so far, It had come so close. If there had been more time to study its alien host, it might not have allowed itself to be expelled. It might not have let the host be distracted. But it was too late now.

Myrtle blinked, as confused as she was relieved. She felt a vague dissatisfaction. She saw the smiling man, and wagged her tail. Maybe he would throw a stick for her. She trotted off to see.

Later, her owners would be amazed to see her being patted by the president on the evening news. They would be even more amazed when a Secret Service agent brought her home.

As for the alien, it dripped down the side of the hydrant and collected in a little puddle on the sidewalk, cooking in the sun.

"Drink me," it called over and over again. "Drink me!"

But nobody did.

# THE 1970S MUST DIE!

## ROBERT JESCHONEK

*Robert Jeschonek continues his streak of being in every issue of* Pulphouse Fiction Magazine. *I wanted to buy this story the moment I read the title. And then I read the opening paragraph and was hooked.*

*I was an adult in the 1970s. Got married twice in the 1970s. I was the editor for this story, that's for sure.*

*Robert's stories have appeared in dozens of magazines and he has published dozens of novels as well. He has even worked for DC Comics and early in his career sold me a couple stories when I was editing for Star Trek at Pocket Books. He seems to be able to do it all. And to see all the amazing projects he has done, check out his website at https://www.robertjeschonek.com/*

# THE 1970S MUST DIE!

## ROBERT JESCHONEK

No sooner had Agent Lyssa Bonne Nuit darted through the hail of dial telephones and cheese whiz than her chrono-bike raced into a blizzard of Saturday Morning Cartoons.

Instantly, the lilac-skinned woman in the black carbon mesh jumpsuit was engulfed in churning waves of bright primary colors and limited animation. Images of snickering dogs, teenagers, and superheroes moved stiffly around her as she worked the bike's controls with all six hands, fighting to catch up with her quarry...and the treasure she'd chased halfway across the time-realm of When, all the way from the Everarium.

Suddenly, the giant image of a singing cartoon duck and rabbit appeared in front of Lyssa, jarring her attention...but she didn't slow down. The duck's orange bill seemed to swallow her whole as she squeezed the accelerator and bolted through it.

Zipping out the other side, she saw the burst of speed had been worth it. Pyre Ransom, the object of Lyssa's pursuit, was up ahead, hurtling through a rippling curtain of colorful characters—everything from cartoon bears to cavemen to cats and mice.

Pyre zoomed through it without ever looking back. The fugitive—a gold-skinned female android—was focused only on getting away with her prize: the decade dubbed the 1970s by the extinct species known as humanity.

Agent Lyssa was determined to take that prize away from her at any cost. Its containment cartridge was steadily leaking Saturday Morning Cartoons and other sociocultural flotsam from the 70s, causing havoc in the skies and streets of When.

One more burst of speed, and Lyssa tore through the last rippling curtain of cartoon characters in Pyre's wake. This time, she emerged in a storm of streakers—images of naked human beings sprinting through the silvery mist, body parts bouncing wildly with each loping step. Every one of them was grinning, an expression Lyssa had come to associate with human joy or pleasure...though she had never met a human and never would.

Because every human being had died out ages ago.

The human race lived on only as echoes in the Yesterplex of the Timekeepers—hyper-rez snapshots of life on ancient planet Earth captured at intervals throughout human history. These flawless log files recorded every detail of entire decades on compact cartridges like the one in Pyre's pack.

These decade backups—known as decalogs—were stored in the vaults of the Everarium, a repository considered impenetrable until Pyre's daring heist. Decalogs were priceless beyond all words, especially in the case of a species like humanity that no longer existed.

As the streakers bounded past with organs flopping, Lyssa fought to stay on track. She lost sight of Pyre up ahead because the gaggle was so dense—also because she was distracted by seeing so many life-size humans in one place. Over the years, Lyssa had studied humans at length and formed a special bond with their long-gone species. They had something in common, something she connected with on a very deep level.

As a final surge of virtual streakers poured past, meaty bodies jiggling, Lyssa saw she had a clear shot at Pyre, who was less than fifty meters away.

Yanking the Was-Gun from the holster strapped around her thorax, Lyssa pointed it at her golden target. Quickly taking aim, she squeezed the trigger, unleashing the weapon's payload.

The barrel of the gun disgorged a deadly Past-Blast—a roiling mass of temporal detritus sucked from multiple eras of a chosen species' history. As always, Lyssa's own sidearm was set to tap the past of humankind, the object of her greatest fascination.

The ejected mass hurtled through the mist, a cyclone of ancient Roman swords, World War II machine guns, furiously kick-stomping boots, and exploding Molotov cocktails. The mass was moving so fast, it looked as if it would consume Pyre's bike at any second.

Before that could happen, though, Pyre dove from its path and swooped away. The Past-Blast spun harmlessly off through the mist, its howling/booming/clanging growing fainter with each passing second.

Cursing, Lyssa dove after Pyre, pouring on as much speed as she could. Still staying out of reach, Pyre dropped into a bank of crimson clouds, kicking up bright red wisps in her wake.

Only when Lyssa plunged through those same clouds and burst out the other side did she realize where the thief was headed.

"Oh no." The violet antennae and feathery pink cilia on her head flickered madly. "She's heading for the *Yesterplex!*"

————

When you lived and worked in When, as Lyssa did, the past, present, and future blurred together. Memories, current experience, and premonitions intermingled, because When existed outside normal spacetime.

It was a phenomenon you had to learn to block or at least manage if you wanted to live anything like a normal life...but there were some things you could never narrow down to present sight alone. Some things were so filled with power and importance, they *forced* you to see them from all time angles. They *intruded*, they *insisted*, they *expanded*.

Which was exactly how the Yesterplex was to Lyssa. Gazing down at its lofty silver spire in the present day, she also remembered the first time she'd seen it, the first time she'd come to When as a child.

*Welcome to the place that is both of and beyond all time.* Those had been the words of Skulk, the red-scaled spider-thing who had brought her here from her home planet of Hinjeri VII. *It is here you will be cared for and learn to care for all the ages in turn.*

The whole time Skulk had talked, Lyssa had simply

stared at that giant spire jutting skyward, a tower that had seemed to her to symbolize the end of everything she'd known.

Her parents had been so proud when she'd been chosen to study at the Yesterplex to become a Timekeeper. Lyssa had been so excited when Skulk had come to Hinjeri VII to get her...but it hadn't lasted. Near the end of the journey to When, terrible news had come in over the radio; Lyssa had learned her entire world had been destroyed by a catastrophe. That was when her excitement had turned to anguish, her hope to fear, her dreams to nightmares.

Because, for the rest of her life, she'd be known as the last survivor of her extinct species, the Hinj.

*These are the halls of the Yesterplex,* she remembered Skulk saying, pointing at the vast figure eight structure sprawling around the base of the silver spire. *The Timekeepers dwell within, preserving yesterday, today, and tomorrow.*

Years later, Lyssa had become a Timekeeper herself. She had poured herself into it, giving it everything she had to make up for what she'd lost. She had never regretted it, either —except when she'd discovered the limits of her commission. Except when she'd discovered the true depths of hopelessness into which she could fall.

————

When Lyssa touched down at the base of the great silver spire, she saw Pyre's chrono-bike discarded on the golden pavement there. Pyre herself was nowhere to be seen...but the route she'd taken was obvious.

The ground-level doors to the Yesterplex gaped nearby,

blown open by something that had left scorch marks and shattered glass in its wake. The bodies of dozens of armed and armored Timekeepers lay all around it, unmoving—victims of the golden-skinned android's great strength, blinding speed, and arsenal of weapons. The security here had been no better able to resist her than that of the great repository of the Everarium.

Leaping from her bike, Lyssa hurried forward, stopping only to check the pulse of one of the Timekeeper guards. He was unconscious, not dead, which was a relief—but she knew she didn't have time to check all the rest. Her most important task right now was catching up to Pyre, then finding out—and stopping—whatever it was she intended to do next.

The nature of Pyre's plans was still a mystery to her, though. All Lyssa knew for sure was it was no accident that Pyre had gone straight to the Yesterplex after stealing the 70s decalog from the Everarium.

Drawing four sidearms, Lyssa charged inside the building, right into the aftermath of another battle. Dozens more Timekeepers were scattered across the floor of the vast lobby, every one of them battered, still, and silent.

Red emergency lights flashed, and sirens shrieked at deafening levels. Though Lyssa knew there were many more Timekeepers in the complex, they hadn't arrived yet to pick up where their defeated comrades had left off in stopping the intruder.

Lyssa wasn't about to wait for them. Guns at the ready, she ran into the central corridor dead ahead, dodging the bodies of guards that were strewn underfoot.

As she raced down the gleaming central corridor, Lyssa tapped a lump on one wrist and called up a virtual status map to guide her. The blinking red blip that represented Pyre was only a few turns ahead and registered as stationary, holding position at least for the moment. Maybe she'd finally been cornered by Timekeeper security?

Heart pounding, Lyssa raced toward her target, resolving to fulfill her two-part orders from Timekeeper Command: to stop Pyre from attaining whatever goal she had in mind and to retrieve the decalog intact.

The second part could prove to be tricky, as the decalog cartridge was already damaged and leaking flotsam. Yet again, as she closed in on Pyre, bits of the 1970s sailed around her. Cans of Billy Beer pelted past like they'd been shot from a cannon, then Richard Nixon heads and platform shoes with towering heels.

As she rounded the final corner, fingers twitching against the triggers of her Was-Guns, the image of a platoon of Viet Cong soldiers, all in black, came howling toward her, firing away with Kalashnikov rifles. The troops were just temporal backwash, a trick of the light, but they startled her, and she hesitated.

That was just enough time for Pyre to unload a blast from her Was-Gun. A howling cyclonic bolus of barbarian axes, rabid wolves, berserker warriors, and laser-equipped airborne drones came spinning after the Viet Cong, punching straight toward Lyssa.

As that raging plume of death bore toward her, Lyssa felt again the sense of doom and horror she had known on the day her species had died…and the day they'd died a *second* time, all because of her.

———

A
s a child and then a young woman, Lyssa had been fascinated by the decalog repository of the Everarium.

*You see before you the archived eras of every sentient species in the galaxy, alive or dead.* On Lyssa's first visit there, Skulk had swept one bristly black leg from side to side to encompass a seemingly endless vault with all its sky-high ranks of crystalline drawers. *The past and present of intelligent life is preserved here for all posterity.*

*Even my own people?* little Lyssa had asked. *Even the Hinji of Hinjeri VII?*

*Of course.* Skulk had skittered to an access kiosk and typed on a keyboard there. A virtual image of Lyssa's home planet had spun to life above the kiosk, then zoomed in to show the long-dead populace going about their daily business. *As long as this recording exists, their legacy will survive.*

Another day, Skulk had shown her around the Yesterplex, introducing her to the multitude of sophisticated devices there —like the Chrono-Rebooter, which could restore a decade from a decalog backup if the timestream for an era became corrupted.

*This powerful instrument can undo the damage of warped or ruined time by rebooting an archived era from the Everarium,* Skulk had explained. *Yet it can only be handled by the most experienced of Timekeepers in the most delicate of ways. To do otherwise risks a chain reaction that could ravage all eternity.*

Lyssa had nodded with an expression of full understanding, but all she'd really heard was the part about rebooting an era from the Everarium.

Starting that day, she'd worked out a plan, always keeping it to herself. If she'd said a word to Skulk, she'd been sure the great spider would have turned her in to the Timekeeper authorities.

But months later, Lyssa had found herself wishing that Skulk had known about the plan after all. Maybe then, someone would have stopped her from "borrowing" a few key decades of Hinji history from the Everarium, then sneaking them into the Yesterplex. Maybe she wouldn't have used the Chrono-Rebooter to try to reboot Hinji history into the space-time continuum and restart her dead species.

Maybe then, Lyssa wouldn't have made a drastic miscalculation that destroyed the stolen decalogs, wiping out decades' worth of backups that could never be recovered.

And a chunk of Hinji history would not have been forever erased and all hope of resurrecting her people as she'd known them extinguished because of something she had done.

————

Six arms whirling, Lyssa battled her way through the Past-Blast from Pyre's Was-Gun, repelling every axe-hack, wolf bite, laser blast, and sword slash with speed and grace.

By the time she was done, the blast components were scattered and defused, bleeding out on the floor or skidding along the walls or ceiling. Tossing away an axe she'd seized, she spun to face Pyre, only to find she was long gone by then.

Cursing, Lyssa pulled up the virtual map and broke into a

run. According to the map, Pyre was already deep in the tunnels leading to the core of the Yesterplex.

Knowing Pyre was heading for the core was enough to make Lyssa run faster. She could only imagine the kind of damage someone like Pyre could do in there with a loaded decalog in her possession.

Pyre certainly knew her way around the Yesterplex and its array of instrumentation. A former Timekeeper, she'd gone rogue for reasons unknown, putting her skills to use in breaking into the Everarium, stealing the 70s human decalog, and bringing it here.

Rounding one bend after another in pursuit of her quarry, Lyssa kept four Was-Gun pistols in hand and ready to fire. She kept her antennae and cilia focused ahead, probing the air for any scent, vibration, or chemical reaction that might signal danger.

But when the danger finally came, she wasn't ready for it.

Racing into an open intersection centered on a statue of Hojo Cahoot—founder of the Yesterplex and Timekeepers—Lyssa was struck by a sudden wave of future sight. She fore-membered a distant tomorrow in which the spot where she now stood was a barren plain with the smoking rubble of the Yesterplex scattered across it.

Stunned, she staggered to a stop, overwhelmed by the smell of death and the shrieks of the dying all around her. Carrion birds wheeled overhead, their great wings beating, and scavenger vermin scampered among the corpses.

Would *this* be the result of whatever grand plan Pyre had in mind? Would the destruction of the Yesterplex and the slaughter of the Timekeepers be her masterstroke?

Suddenly, Lyssa heard a familiar voice from somewhere

nearby, begging for death. Even before she turned to see the source, she recognized it all too well.

She recognized it as *her* voice...and in that instant, she knew the forememory was false.

Pinching her eyes shut, she shook off the vision. Trained agent that she was, she knew a fake when she saw one and how to fend it off. Future memories were always experienced through your own senses, from your future self's point of view. If, when experiencing a foremembrance, you heard your voice as part of the mix, but you weren't actually doing the talking, it was never the real thing.

It was nothing but an *aftermine* in action, a device that generated false visions of the future.

Opening her eyes, she saw the nightmare future was gone. Looking further, she saw a mirrored sphere, no more than four inches in diameter, tucked between the webbed feet of the statue of Hojo Cahoot.

Sprinting forward, she crushed the aftermine sphere with the heel of her boot, smashing it to tiny pieces. Then, hoping she hadn't been too long delayed, she bolted down the corridor that led to the core.

A s Lyssa charged into the core—the cavernous central chamber underneath the spire of the Yesterplex—she came upon another dozen unconscious Timekeepers on the floor. Apparently, they'd made a last stand against Pyre...and failed to stop her.

Beyond the bodies sprawled concentric rings of alabaster white partitions and alcoves—the mazelike command complex of the core. Searching those convoluted warrens for Pyre could take hours...if not for the very clear sign of her exact location that Lyssa instantly spotted.

A giant yellow circle rose like a sun near the middle of the core, its massive face marked with a simple smile in thick, black strokes. Student of humanity that she was, Lyssa instantly recognized the classic smiley face symbol of the 1970s.

Weaving through the command complex, she no longer needed to watch Pyre's blip on the virtual map. The place was like a maze, but the enormous smiley face was easy to follow.

Lyssa braced herself as she closed in, expecting another trap or trick. Her last few turns were uneventful, though, and she reached the open plaza at the middle of the core without incident.

At the plaza's center, a massive machine hung from above, a silver-plated cone extending high into the cavity within the Yesterplex's spire. The cone was covered in twinkling, multi-colored lights and tapered to a fine point ending a meter or so from the floor. Standing there, operating a virtual control console encircling the cone's tip, was Pyre Ransom herself.

Seeing her there like that sent a shiver through Lyssa's body. She knew that machine well—*too* well—from past experience.

Pyre was using the very same Chrono-Rebooter that Lyssa had used to accidentally gut the recorded history of her people so many years ago.

———

L yssa slowly approached, but Pyre didn't look up from her work. Her golden fingers flickered over the virtual controls, causing changes in the patterns of blinking lights on the conelike device.

When Lyssa was ten meters away, however, Pyre told her not to come any closer. "I'll put you down, I swear," she said calmly.

Lyssa stopped and lowered her guns. "So you like humanity's 1970s period too, huh?"

As she said it, red, white, and blue streamers and fireworks exploded in midair above them, residue of the United States of America's Bicentennial celebration in 1976.

"Sure," Pyre said without looking up. "Just not in the way you think."

Lyssa knew she should take a shot at gunning her down; the potential danger of letting her keep working on the Rebooter was high. But part of her was holding back until she understood better what Pyre's plan was. "So are you going to try bringing them back? The 1970s of humankind?"

"Maybe you should mind your own business." Pyre's fingers flew through a complex sequence of controls, and all the lights on the Chrono-Rebooter ignited at once.

"Are you sure you don't want any help?" asked Lyssa.

"*You* wouldn't be much help. You lost your user rights to this thing *ages* ago."

Lyssa scowled. Pyre was right; the Timekeepers had permanently revoked her rights to use the Rebooter after the Hinj incident. It was the one piece of equipment in the entire Yesterplex that she wasn't allowed to use.

"Pretty sure *you're* not supposed to have user rights,

either," said Lyssa. "The Timekeepers deprovisioned you from all systems as soon as you quit the corps."

"True," said Pyre, "but I was smart enough to buy an access hack from an unscrupulous insider."

"Good for you."

Suddenly, Pyre reached into her pocket, and Lyssa tensed. Pyre drew out a cylindrical cartridge the length of a cigar, made of a clear material and churning inside with red, yellow, and green mist.

Lyssa knew instantly what it was, what it had to be—the 1970s decalog—and she guessed Pyre was ready to deploy it.

Leaping into action, she charged Pyre. Shooting would have been too risky; she didn't want another destroyed decade on her conscience, especially from the history of humanity.

As Lyssa sprang, Pyre whipped out her Was-Gun. She got off one shot, but it was wild, and Lyssa put hands on her before she could fire another...*five* hands, to be exact.

Her sixth hand landed on Pyre's hand that was wrapped around the 70s decalog. Maybe she squeezed too hard, though, or the shock of the impact triggered a reflexive contraction of Pyre's grip.

Because as soon as Lyssa made contact with the cartridge, a blinding white light flared, and she was gone.

———

Lyssa blinked away the white light and the black spots it had left raging in her eyes. Little by little, her vision cleared, and she was able to make out the details of her surroundings.

It was then she realized she wasn't inside the Yesterplex

anymore. She was somewhere different, somewhere unfamiliar, somewhere...

*Grander.*

She stood on a hilltop, gazing out at a valley below. The valley was filled with trees, a carpet of emerald rippling in the warm breeze of a sunny summer day.

What interested Lyssa the most, though, were the occupants of the skies overhead. Massive crystal spheres hung high above the valley, glittering in the midday sun. Through the skin of these colossal objects, Lyssa could see the dance of light and movement that signified life—sentient life capable of building such grand structures and miraculously keeping them aloft.

"Spectacular, aren't they?"

At the sound of Pyre's voice, Lyssa jerked her head around to see the android standing behind her.

"The cities of paradise, circa 1975," said Pyre, smiling serenely. "Each one full of people living to their maximum potential."

Lyssa scowled. Her instinct was to grab and restrain Pyre, but she held herself back...for the moment, at least. "Where *exactly* is this? Where are we?"

"Inside the 1970s decalog," explained Pyre. "Our *minds* only. Think of it as a peek inside the cartridge I stole."

"The 1970s *where?*" asked Lyssa. "Because it sure isn't the *Earth* of *humanity*."

"Oh, but it is." Pyre chuckled and stepped away, moving forward on the hilltop. "I assure you, it very much *is.*"

Just then, a low-flying aircraft buzzed the hill, and Lyssa ducked. The craft zoomed away without making a sound, its oval fuselage tipped with a long, pointed nose like a needle.

Vents on its backside glowed bright blue and shimmered with what looked like heat ripples.

"That is *not* a human-built aircraft from 1970s Earth." Lyssa stared at other ships in the distance, zipping around and between the crystalline spheres. "*None* of them are."

"*All* of them are." Pyre spread her arms wide to take it all in. "Every last one of them."

Lyssa frowned, struggling to understand. Airborne craft of many shapes and sizes swooped and darted among the spheres, threading from one to the next across the busy blue sky. Little satellites revolved around the spheres as well, often narrowly avoiding collisions with each other, with aircraft, with birds...and with human beings engaged in unaided flight.

Humans flew in and out of the spheres with grace, banking and looping and soaring as if they'd been born to it. As far as Lyssa could see, there were no signs of jetpacks or antigravity tech anywhere on them.

Lyssa was amazed...then annoyed. "This is some kind of elaborate illusion. You've trapped me in a multisensory deepfake."

"But I haven't," Pyre said calmly. "This is recorded reality from Earth in the 1970s...the 1970s *as they were meant to be.*"

Lyssa's frown deepened. "Enough of this. End the simulation."

"It's no simulation," said Pyre.

Lyssa grabbed Pyre's gold-skinned arm. "You can't *save* yourself with *trickery*. You are going to *pay* for your *crimes*."

"Haven't you ever wondered?" Pyre shook off Lyssa's grip and sat down on the grassy peak. "Haven't you wondered why humanity died out so soon? Why things went downhill so fast for such a promising species?"

It was indeed a question Lyssa had asked herself many times, though she wouldn't give Pyre the satisfaction of knowing that. "Species die out. There isn't always a sensible explanation."

"But there is this time."

"What do *you* know about them?" snapped Lyssa.

"Everything." Pyre looked up at her with a grim smile. "Humans *made* me."

Lyssa gaped at her, surprised.

"Human built me, and those like me, to outlive them," said Pyre, "and I have. And now I will correct an injustice that was visited upon them millennia ago...because I can.

"Because all I need to do is replace the 1970s as they happened with the *rightful* 1970s...whatever the cost may be."

———

Lyssa well remembered when she'd first discovered the human race of planet Earth.

As a young trainee Timekeeper in the Everarium (before her ill-fated attempt to resurrect the Hinji), she'd been obsessed with viewing the decalogs of extinct sentient species. She'd made the most of her access to the archives, poring over preserved eras of vanished species for hour upon hour at the expense of her trainee assignments.

So many extinct species had been so much like her own, their tragic stories brimming with lost potential. She'd been fascinated by the multitudes of unsolved mysteries associated with them, the many unknowns left behind in their wakes.

But no species had captured her imagination quite as much as humanity. No species had been so colorful, passionate, and unbridled or had touched her so profoundly with their arts and struggles.

No other species had made her think, if she had to be something other than Hinji, that she would choose to join their ranks.

And no human era had spoken to her so clearly as the 1970s. The thrilling music, flashy fashion, and larger-than-life celebrities had excited her. The search for meaning in an off-kilter world was much like her own search for identity in the realm of When.

The 70s had been such a big deal to Lyssa that they had figured prominently in her own rogue scheme with the Chrono-Rebooter. Originally, she'd planned to bring back humanity after raising the Hinji...and she'd known all along, if she'd gotten that far, that she would have started with the 70s.

It was an obsession she had never grown out of. It was why she had pursued Pyre with such determination when other Timekeepers had fallen by the wayside. It was why she'd come so far and fought so hard.

And it was why now, instead of taking swift action to do her duty upon getting an inkling of Pyre's true intentions, she listened to what the android was saying.

————————

A light breeze wafted over the peak as Lyssa sat cross-legged beside Pyre. Paradise went on around them, its wonders amazing to behold...but Lyssa found her gaze locked on the android's, attached as if by magnets.

"How can there be a *rightful* 1970s?" asked Lyssa. "How can there be anything but history as we know it?"

"Long ago, history was sabotaged," said Pyre. "By those who feared humanity would *surpass* or *destroy* them. A decade was removed from human history, the decade of humankind's greatest renaissance, the ascendance that should have come on the heels of the age of idealism and creativity in the 1960s."

"The 70s were removed?" Only among Timekeepers of When would such a question be asked so matter-of-factly.

Pyre nodded. "And replaced with a very different decade in which a renaissance never happened. An era of selfishness and silly obsessions, a time of conflict and crisis and drift. A flawed decade that gave rise to the forces that robbed humanity of its golden age and accelerated a doom that should never have come."

"That's not true!" snapped Lyssa. She hated hearing her precious 70s denigrated like that. "The 70s may not have been perfect, but *no* decade ever is."

"They weren't what they *could* have been," said Pyre. "What they *should* have been."

Lyssa felt the urge to punch her in the face. "According to whom?"

"According to the one person who *lived through* the original version, came to When before the timeline changed, and still survives to *this day*." Pyre tapped her chest with an index finger. "According to *me*."

Lyssa felt her anger draining away. She gazed at Pyre as if seeing her for the first time.

Now she knew—if Pyre was telling the truth—how she could be so certain that an alternate 1970s had replaced an original version populated by an enlightened humanity. Now she knew—again, if Pyre wasn't lying—how the promising human species had died out so prematurely.

It was all thanks to the Timekeepers and their technological wonders.

Still, Lyssa had trouble wrapping her head around it all. "But the Timekeepers are sworn not to tamper with the time-lines. It's our greatest oath."

"Certain circumstances may supersede that oath," said Pyre. "Such as whispers of the threat one species may present if allowed to reach full bloom. The *status quo* must *always* be preserved." Pyre grinned and held out her hand, where the mist-filled cylinder of the decalog cartridge remained—or at least a mental manifestation of it. "Unless someone is stupid enough to keep a *backup* copy of the over-written *original*."

Lyssa frowned. "But I thought the stolen decalog was from the *accepted* 1970s. The whole time I chased you, it was leaking smiley faces, streakers, Viet Cong soldiers—all sorts of 70s odds and ends."

Pyre shook her head. "That was all virtual trickery, projected by me to hide the true nature of my mission." She pressed her chin, opened her mouth, and the image of a 70s game show host with shaggy brown hair, a long microphone, and a powder blue leisure suit with white buck shoes appeared in midair between them. When Pyre closed her

146

mouth, the image disappeared. "The decalog only ever contained the essence of the *rightful* human 70s."

"Which you want to use for a reboot?"

"To overwrite the replacement 70s, yes." When Pyre smiled, her bright red eyes sparkled. "Make the golden age a reality again as it was meant to be. Give humanity a second chance to overcome its premature extinction."

Lyssa's antennae twitched with strong emotion. What Pyre was saying—she didn't hate the idea. But there were issues the android hadn't mentioned yet.

"If you do this—it'll change more than *human* history, won't it?" asked Lyssa. "Assuming humanity is reborn, the ripple effects will affect everyone the resurrected human species comes in contact with. Will the Chrono-Rebooter even let that happen?"

"I believe so," said Pyre. "With the right *minds* injected into the mix to guide the process." She grinned. "Say, a human-built synthetic who can interface with the rebooter's A.I. and a female organic who can convince it that rules are made to be broken."

Lyssa's eyes widened. Pyre was talking about *her*.

———

For a long moment, Lyssa just stared at Pyre, wondering if this was what they'd been moving toward all along.

Did Pyre know how she felt about humanity? Was it possible the android had been pulling her in this direction from the start, for just this purpose?

Either way, a proposition had been made that could change everything—a proposition with an extremely uncertain outcome—yet Lyssa found she could not dismiss it out of hand.

"I still don't understand what makes you think I can help," she said.

"Using my own computerized mind, I have calculated that the rebooter's A.I. will more likely respond favorably when interfacing with someone like you," said Pyre. "Someone who knows what it's like when you don't *have* a chance to bring back the people you've lost. Someone who understands from first-hand experience that the *absence* of those who matter can send out just as many ripples as their *presence* can.

"Someone who once used that very rebooter to try to bring someone else back—and now wants to give both of them a chance to make up for that failure."

"I see." Lyssa was surprised at how sensible it all sounded, though one question kept nagging at her. "So how do I know you're not lying?"

Pyre frowned. "About what?"

"About everything," said Lyssa. "How do I know that any of this is the truth?"

"Because of all this, of course." Pyre gestured at the scene stretched out before them—the great glittering crystalline spheres hovering over the emerald forest.

"Which could be nothing but an illusion," said Lyssa.

"But listen." Pyre leaned toward her, one golden index finger raised instructively. "Can you take the chance that's all it is? If I'm right—which I am—but you let me fail, can you bear it? Can you live with yourself, knowing you could have brought back humanity but didn't?"

Lyssa didn't answer. Pyre's story was strangely persuasive, appealing to her longtime love of humanity and her desire to resurrect that species—but part of her held fast, refusing to be convinced of anything by the fugitive thief. No Timekeeper worth her salt would fall for a line of bullshit like the one she was hearing, and she knew it.

At least that was how she felt before the next question Pyre asked.

"Also, can you live with yourself if this is all true, and you let it fail...knowing success could have led to more than one change?" Pyre folded her hands together, her fingers interwoven. "What if humanity's destiny is connected to *another* destiny that is not at first obvious?"

"Another destiny?"

Pyre shrugged. "Who's to say that bringing humanity back won't bring back someone else?"

Lyssa's heart pounded as she considered the implications. Her doubts and fears began to melt away.

"Do you...do you know this for a fact?" she asked. "That someone else could be restored by such a change?"

"I do not know it for a fact," said Pyre. "But can you bear to take the chance that it won't happen?"

Lyssa turned away, thinking and watching the view of paradise. Multicolored beams of lights blazed from the city-spheres, splashing over the emerald forest and sapphire sky. Music like wind chimes and whalesong played from speakers unseen, echoing in the distance.

It was beautiful. Was it worth leaping into the unknown for, though? Solely on its own merits? She couldn't seem to make that argument to herself.

But that last thing that Pyre had said, she could not ignore. It kept running through her mind, again and again.

*Can you bear to take the chance that it won't happen?*

"If we do this, what will happen to us?" she asked suddenly. "After it's all over, whatever the outcome...what happens to us?"

Pyre shrugged and reached out with the decalog cartridge in her hand. "Does it matter? Will it change your answer?"

Just like that, Lyssa realized she had made up her mind. It was not lost on her that it was the most impulsive decision she had made since trying to reboot the history of the Hinji three decades ago. "No." Smiling, she folded all six of her hands around the cartridge in Pyre's grip. "No, it won't."

Then, she felt Pyre squeeze tightly, crushing the cartridge, and the glorious vision of the rightful 1970s dissolved in whirling clouds of phosphorescent vapor.

————————

Elsewhere, Elsewhen:
Silver and sleek, the star-skiff full of humans swooped into the atmosphere of the pink-and-purple planet. Gleaming in the light of the planet's triple suns, the little craft swooped gracefully toward the surface, approaching the celebration of a momentous occasion.

"This is the Earth skiff *Impresario.*" The little craft was just as lovely on the inside, its bright cockpit fitted with silver consoles studded with blinking, multicolored controls. The pilot, Murphy—a willowy woman with short red hair and a pale blue uniform with silver piping—spoke into a mic that floated in front of her lush red lips. "Requesting permission to land."

"Only if that *admiral* of yours isn't aboard!" the man on the other end of the call said teasingly. "Though Todd Chamberlain's so *old* and *frail* these days, I'll bet he had to stay in orbit on the *mothership* and take his *nap!*"

Grinning, the gray-haired man in a navy blue uniform who shared the cockpit with Murphy leaned over from the co-pilot's seat to speak into the mic. "You think I'd miss out on *today?* Forget it, Mr. President!"

The man on the line chuckled. "It's only our five-hundred-year anniversary, Todd! No need for a big man like yourself to come down off your high horse and mingle with us *little people.*"

"I wouldn't miss it for anything, President Prine," said Admiral Chamberlain, who looked middle-aged though he was much, much older. "Any chance to rub your nose in what I did for you, I'll *jump* at it."

"*You?* It was all *you*, now?" Prine said with mock outrage.

"Who's gonna say any different?" asked Chamberlain.

"Have you forgotten my people can live to be a thousand years old?" said Prine. "You *humans* are lucky to live *half* that!"

"Whatever." Chamberlain winked at Murphy. "You people have a funny way of acting grateful, don't you?"

"We won't kiss your asses, if that's what you mean." Prine laughed. "But come on down anyway if you like. We won't stop you."

With that, the communication ended.

And Chamberlain and Murphy howled with laughter.

"What a character!" said Murphy.

"I love that guy!" Chamberlain slapped his knee. "He's just as hilarious as he was 500 years ago when we saved his goddamn planet!"

Later, after the skiff had landed and the ceremonies had begun, Chamberlain marched solemnly over the purple ground of the planet, flanked by several human dignitaries in their best formal attire. Up ahead, a dais waited, adorned with pink, violet, and lilac colored flowers.

Flickering video panels hung in midair, replaying scenes from the historic events of half a millennium ago. On one, Chamberlain saw his old vessel, the Earthship *Intensity*, descending to the surface for the first time. On the next panel over, Chamberlain's science team worked with an array of elaborate equipment on the planet's surface, confirming the ominous readings they had first detected from orbit.

On the next panel, Chamberlain and his crew made one of the least auspicious first contacts ever with the local inhabitants, informing them of their findings. *Hi, nice to meet you! By the way, your world is about to explode.*

Then, on the final panel, the humans and locals were working side by side, constructing a gargantuan device that would stop the explosion and save the world. All thanks to the high-tech ingenuity and altruism that had thrived on Earth since the start of humanity's golden age in the 1970s, two thousand years ago.

Chamberlain felt a surge of pride and nostalgia as he approached the dais where the leading lights of the planet waited to mark the great occasion. Before he could set one foot on the dais, however, his old friend, President Prine, ran forward.

And threw his six purple arms around him in a bear hug.

"It is so *good* to see you, my friend!" Prine leaned back, his beaded violet antennae bobbing with pure joy. The feathery pink cilia on his purple head and neck fluttered and danced as he beamed. "You have been away from Hinjeri VII and the Hinji people for far too long!"

"Tell me about it!" Tears rolled down Chamberlain's cheeks. People were watching—whole planets of them, via the media —and he didn't give a damn.

"Thank you again, my friend," said Prine. "If not for you, this place would not exist. None of us would."

"I've always had a feeling," said Chamberlain, reveling in the embrace of his Hinji friend as the galaxy looked on. "I've always had a feeling that somehow, it works both ways."

# FROM THE GOOD OLD DAYS

## JAMES GOTAAS

*James Gotaas's story is a very original science fiction story with a character you just want to spend more time with. And it is set in a world that I personally hope James writes more stories and novels in.*

*James' stories are always fun and different and I look forward to having many more of them in Pulphouse. And I have a hunch readers will start looking forward to them as well.*

# FROM THE GOOD OLD DAYS

## JAMES GOTAAS

O ur starship juddered back into normal spacetime.
As usual, my stomach juddered back into normal spacetime somewhere around my tonsils, and I struggled against the urgent need to spew its sour contents out over my jumpsuit and into the control room.

I gingerly shook my head, trying to clear away the uncomfortable visual after-effects of emergence back into real-space, everything appearing slightly doubled and wavering. I twisted slightly to look across the two meters to where the captain, my boss Fraddek, sat calmly at his station. As always, he appeared completely unaffected by the transition that twisted my nervous and digestive systems into knots.

After a few seconds, I managed to focus on the virtual screen hanging before my eyes. It displayed the K4 primary and the projected orbits of its planets, looking down on the plane of the system's ecliptic from fifteen billion kilometers above the star.

Another fifteen seconds or so elapsed and the *Leap Twice*

*Before You Look* announced, "Destination five confirmed by spectroscopic analysis. Initiating passive scans for planets and active installations."

A couple of deep breaths, another cautious shake of my head, and I finally felt up to speaking. "How long?"

"As you know, Bob, it takes as long as it takes," the ship snapped.

I cut off a retort. Even after a year, the ship didn't like me. I had to confess that I returned the favor with extra compliments. I'd have happily traded the AI for a basket of over-ripe hackberries. A small basket. But I wasn't the owner or boss.

I just looked across the deck at Fraddek. "Can't you just order the *Leap* to accept me?"

The short, stocky alien giggled. "I've tried. It's stubborn."

"What's it got against me, anyway?"

"Nothing personal, but it just can't ignore the fact that you're human."

"So what has *Leap* got against humans?"

"You mean aside from the fact that your First Empire caused a lot of chaos and destruction among the rest of the civilizations in this part of the galaxy, your species has obnoxious social habits, and you emit strange and unpleasant odors?"

Aside from the fact that he was my boss, I couldn't actually argue with his perception of humans. It was a view generally accepted even by our alien allies. Hell, it was accepted by some humans living away off Earth. Still, I protested, "The ship can't even smell me!"

*Leap* couldn't pass that up. "I have a complete array of internal sensors. You stink."

So it didn't like any humans. I'd spent a big part of my

adult life outside the human reaches, and this wasn't the first time I'd come across such sentiments. It still rankled.

I muttered, "I'm surprised you rescued me from that mob." A year ago, an angry crowd of semi-bovine aliens had been unhappy about my narrow escape from execution. They'd been intent on finishing the job, legally or otherwise, and were in the process when Fraddek had come to my rescue. Not only had he saved me, he'd even offered me a job that I desperately needed.

The boss shrugged. "I made a lot of money betting on you with that execution. Anyway, I don't mind humans. I've made a profit from their behaviour over the years. And the First Empire never reached as far as my home world."

"But how did *Leap* get so anti-human? It can't be that old."

"*Leap* is proud that some of its core code can be traced back to warships that fought against your First Empire."

There wasn't much I could say to that. I settled for sulking.

*Leap* finally spoke up. "Passive scans completed. Initial result: two terrestrial-class planets, two Jovian-class, three ice giants. No active installations detected. No ships detected. Permission to initiate active scans?"

Another voice echoed across the command deck. "That tickled."

We both looked up at the side display linked to the third crewmember, currently resting on standby in the main storage hold.

Fraddek spoke first. "What's that, Zak?"

Zak was an autonomous Weapons Interdiction Intelligent Mobile Protector Platform. A deadly war machine, he'd been freed from military servitude and become a pacifist. He'd also helped rescue me from the mob. "Something just probed me, and it tickled my neutronium toes." And he had a silly sense of humor.

Fraddek stiffened. "*Leap*, did you detect a probe?"

The ship actually hesitated. "There was something, but it wasn't any standard sensor sweep. The closest comparison is a minor gravity wave."

I started to query that but was interrupted by a wave of nausea and the feeling that my body had been swung around violently. The command deck was suddenly totally dark.

Emergency systems flickered on. My stomach started a protest at the sudden absence of our artificial gravity, and the backup lighting left most of the small command deck dim.

Fraddek demanded, "What's going on?"

*Leap* answered, "We have been displaced and our primary energy systems are offline."

"What do you mean displaced?"

"We are no longer at the location of our arrival. Something has moved us elsewhere in the system. Our active scanning systems are blocked, so our actual position is unknown."

Zak piped up, "And I'm being scanned by several different sensor types. None of them match anything in my weapon data banks." After a moment, he went on, "Ouch. It just turned off my weapons systems. That hurts."

Something loud squawked throughout the command deck. It sounded vaguely familiar.

Fraddek reacted first. "Is that a language?"

"Unclear," *Leap* responded.

"Yes," Zak said. "It has a match in my military history banks. It's Old Terran."

Ah, that explained my marginal familiarity. In school, we were still exposed to heroic poetry from the age of the first

Terran explorers – or conquerors, as the rest of the galaxy preferred to call them. Just to be absolutely clear, I asked, "You mean from the First Empire?"

"Yes," Zak responded. "And I'm accessing *Leap's* optical sensors. Confirm we are in the vicinity of a First Empire System Conqueror Class warship."

I carried on. "So this is part of a system invasion fleet?"

Zak gently corrected me. "Bob, this *is* a system invasion fleet. This single ship is more powerful than the full military space fleet of any existing government. Estimated maximum dimension approximately six hundred kilometers, consistent with historical data. According to my records, they were never defeated in overt combat, only ever by stealth and sabotage."

Fraddek spoke up. "Let's forget the history. Can you translate?"

"Perhaps. Probably badly."

Another squawk. It seemed even louder.

I shook my head. "A bad translation may be better than none at all. That sounded … urgent."

*Leap* contributed, "More scans. They are reading my data storage banks."

A staccato voice suddenly rang out, "This is Imperial Ship *Stronger Than Any*. We have now adjusted to your apparent preferred language. You are under interdiction for trespass into an Imperial Protected Zone."

I glanced at Fraddek and whispered, "Is that possible?"

He whispered back, "Apparently. The First Empire was very advanced in terms of weaponry and contact technology. Much of it was lost in the wars of freedom."

The strange voice spoke again. "There is no historical reference for wars of freedom. Based on overlapping data, you are referring to the Great Insurrection, which is still ongoing."

So whispering didn't work as a way of keeping secrets.

The voice continued, "Ship commander: can you provide authentication and authorization?"

Fraddek shook his head. "No. We're not from your Empire."

"Combat Attorney Fraddek Sryl non-Female Third-born of Kornpohlblut, I was speaking to the commander. It is assumed that, since Robert Oliver is not assigned a rank in your databases, he is operating incognito. But operational contingencies now require him to identify himself."

Hell. It thought I was an agent of the First Empire? Which hadn't existed in any meaningful form for almost a thousand years?

I thought fast. I cleared my throat. "I'm not sure that I can do that." Maybe this monster ship would accept an imaginary overriding need for secrecy?

The measured tones of the Imperial ship took on the characteristics of a spokesman for the Apocalypse. "If you cannot provide authentication and authorization, I will have to place your ship and crew in stasis to await judgment by the appropriate authorities."

Oops. I doubted that those authorities actually existed any longer.

Which probably explained the enigma we'd come here to explore – why had three exploration ships vanished in this barren remote area of interstellar space in the past fifty years?

I decided to check. "How many ships are in stasis?"

It seemed to accept my query as legitimate. "Three hundred and sixty-two."

Well, the odds were good that number included the ones we were looking for. And just as good that we would soon be increasing that tally to three hundred and sixty-three.

"Commander?"

Fraddek's polite word dragged me away from the edge of that particular pit of despair. Then I realized what he'd said.

"Uh, yes?"

"I realize that you can't ... disclose your status here. But perhaps if you transferred to the Imperial ship?"

I just stared at him. Had he cracked under the stress? No. Not possible. Not Fraddek, who could outthink and outfight any sapient up to three times the size of his diminutive 2.5 G body. So then what was he thinking?

I didn't have a clue. I finally answered him, "I'm not sure that's a good idea."

In fact, it struck as me a completely bad idea, since there was absolutely no possibility that I could disclose my unfortunately non-existent status wherever I might end up in the damned galaxy.

"It's the only idea," he answered back firmly. His left hand twitched against his tunic and its front panel lit up with the distinctive characters of interstellar trading shorthand: *Only chance. Get aboard. Subvert programming.*

I decided that it was, after all, quite possible that Fraddek had cracked under the stress. *Me* subvert a warship of the First Empire? I had all the technical expertise that my previous job of tramp spaceship cargo steward had required. Which was just about enough to identify the right tabs to swipe on or off on a child-friendly control panel. Beyond that, I struggled to subvert the friendly intentions of my wrist comp.

Then the voice of doom rang out again. "That suggestion is acceptable."

Great. So this awesome system-cracker warship thought I could be more transparent if I were safe in its arms. I figured it had lost its mental gyros sometime in that past thousand years of sitting here waiting for the First Empire to show up again.

On the other hand, what did I have to lose? Flip a coin: heads, I ended up in permanent stasis with everyone else on the *Leap*, tails I ended up killed by a crazy Imperial AI.

Or I could be optimistic. Sometimes the coin would land on its edge.

Sure. Given a few hundred billion years of coin tossing.

OK, toss that coin.

So I said, "I'm ready to come aboard you."

I was really glad we'd arrived before lunch. Otherwise I would have lost it in a very messy and embarrassing way when the *Stronger Than Any* somehow twisted space and took me from within the *Leap* to its own interior. The individual transfer hit me worse than the previous displacement of the *Leap Twice Before Looking*.

I was shivering, partly an aftereffect of the transfer between ships, and partly due to the penetrating cold. I looked around at a huge, dimly-lit space filled with flashing screens and dead people as far as I could see.

It didn't fill me with confidence.

"Are these ... members of your crew?"

The ship's voice echoed around me. "Yes. The last crewmember died 927 years ago."

"Shouldn't you ... have ... buried them, or ... something?"

"Regulations forbid it. That is the proper role of the crew, specifically either the medical staff or emergency triage teams.

Our own systems are not allowed to deal with the remains. We enabled natural preservation through implementation of an internal sub-zero and low-humidity environment."

I shook my head and whispered, "That's insane."

"Not true. I am provably sane. I have triple-redundancy failsafe cognitive systems. I am required to follow standard regulations in the absence of direct orders."

I looked again at all the bodies. "Didn't the last survivors take care of proper procedures for dealing with the dead?"

"Unfortunately, a fatal disease passed through the crew too quickly to allow for that."

I almost choked. "A fatal disease?"

"It was identified as a quasi-viral brain infection. No cure was available after symptoms onset. The captain issued final orders for us to follow. We have followed those orders without fail."

"Was this disease contagious?"

"Extremely so. It was first identified at 19.32, day 121, Imperial Year 2817. The last crewmember died at 08.14, day 122, Imperial Year 2817."

Well, I'd flipped the wrong coin this time. "How long until I show symptoms?"

"You are not infected. Appropriate decontamination procedures have been followed. We would not have brought you aboard otherwise."

Let's just say that I was relieved. I'd have been angry if I thought the damn ship had misled me deliberately, but it was just inhuman logic implemented by a human-created device.

A small drone floated up to me.

The ancient ship spoke again. "We will need biological samples to verify your status."

The drone attached itself to my arm and I felt a sharp sting, followed by an immediate sense of cool numbness. The drone moved away.

Silence reigned for what seemed like forever. Had I failed the test of my status? How could I not have? My biological data wouldn't be in any database this ship might have.

After forever ended, the ship spoke again. "DNA status confirmed. Please proceed to the central command station."

Huh? Just what status did I have?

A green line traced its way from where I was to the station that sat in the middle of the vast expanse. I followed it and reached the station, where a mummified body sat still dressed in what was probably a command-level uniform. I stood staring at the long-dead man.

"Please remove the Captain from the command station."

"What?"

"Please remove the Captain from the command station."

"Do … do I have to? Can't I just stand here?"

"Please remove the Captain from the command station."

Clearly it wasn't going to give up, and it could carry on this farce longer than I could. I leaned forward and gingerly lifted the body from the seat. It was lighter than I expected, probably because so much of the water had gone from the body. I carefully placed the body down on the ring surrounding the station and rubbed my frozen hands together.

"Please sit down in the command station."

Even after manhandling a corpse, I was bothered about taking its place, but I didn't have much choice. So I just followed orders. As I leaned back into the station, it closed around me and a helmet settled onto my head. The ship wavered and flickered around me, then snapped into crystal clarity. I realized that I was experiencing a virtual display input directly to my brain. It was more real than any virtuality I'd ever experienced.

Hell it was more real than my normal experience of reality as filtered through my all too fallible senses.

"You are a 99.08% match to a DNA identification in the Imperial Personnel Database. This satisfies the constraints as set down by Captain Ngoba Lee before he died."

So some unknown ancestor had been in the Imperial forces? As the ship mentioned the dead captain's name, his image appeared before me. His face was drawn and haggard.

"Greetings. If you're seeing this, you're either a member of the Imperial Forces or a descendant. We're so far out of Imperial space that it may be a while before the *Stronger Than Any* is located." He hesitated as a cough racked him. "I can't predict the military or political situation you're facing. *Stronger* is positioned here to serve as a rally point for a secondary front in the event of serious setbacks in the Insurrection. The only thing I know for certain is that the ship needs a captain. That's now you. By my authority as captain and over-system commander, I am hereby appointing you as captain of the Imperial Ship *Stronger Than Any*. The ship will complete the briefing. Good luck."

The image vanished.

The ship took over again. "Do you have questions, Captain Oliver?"

"Uh ..." Did I have questions? Did I have anything but questions? "What's your status?"

"Due to lack of required maintenance, ship systems are only 91% functional. The absence of crew reduces combat effectiveness to approximately 65-73%, dependent on the precise nature of the engagement."

"You mean you can function even without a crew?"

"Affirmative. As stated, with partially reduced combat effectiveness."

I tried to imagine what that would be like. Modern ships had AI control, but ultimately required some sort of sapient crew for full operation and maintenance.

Here I was the crew, and I was as close to totally incompetent as it was possible to be and still be breathing. I swallowed.

"Do you have a briefing for me?"

"We were tasked with maintaining control of this stellar system and assuming command of any Imperial ships that join us, then organizing an appropriate command structure and battle order. Our further activities and mission were to be determined by further orders received either by message drone or ship."

"How many Imperial ships have arrived while you waited?"

"None."

"How about message drones?"

"Three. However, none brought further orders from the Empire."

"So you've received no additional orders since your arrival in this system?"

"That is correct."

"And when was that precisely?"

"Day 63, Imperial Year 2817."

I considered that. The First Empire had ceased to exist just over 900 standard years earlier. I made a stab at converting the First Empire date to our modern calendar. I worked out that the Empire had fallen in that same Imperial year. And that pretty much explained why no further orders had come.

The *wars of freedom* that had ended the First Empire had destroyed virtually all existing interstellar forces, both human and alien. It had also nearly ended intelligent life in our section of space.

It started an interregnum that lasted almost 300 years. Between the effects of physical, biological and software weapons, interstellar civilization had crashed. Nearly eighty per cent of the existing populations had died, along with much of the technological infrastructure. Those alien civilizations that had remained outside the Imperial sphere had survived, but largely possessed more primitive technology bases – which was why the First Empire couldn't be bothered to conquer them in the first place.

The current human so-called empire, the Empire of Ancient Terra, had evolved as a form of defense in the face of massive alien hostility. Humans retained just enough technology to stay a bit ahead of those surrounding aliens as the entire galactic neighborhood moved back toward interstellar travel. The modern empire consisted largely of human-dominant worlds and a small number of alien civilizations that for some reason felt safer in the company of humans.

I wondered about the wisdom of those ancients. Why had they dispatched this system conqueror so far beyond the borders, essentially removing it from the conflict?

I'd never paid much attention to ancient history, and never been at all interested in any version of a human empire, past or present. Like most of my peers during school, I'd been slightly embarrassed by the so-called patriotism of the establishment. I'd always felt even more embarrassed by the stories of the harsh rule of the First Empire, which had given humans a bad name that stuck even now.

I wasn't certain, but I had to believe that this ship would have made a massive difference to any battle. Why send it here?

I couldn't even guess. Then again, it didn't really matter now. It was here, and we were here, and that was a major problem.

"Ship?"

"Please refer to me as *Stronger*."

"Uh, right. What happens now?"

"Given the time elapsed since our arrival in this system, it seems unlikely that any further orders will be forthcoming. In that case, our activities will be determined by general orders and the decisions of the crew."

"You mean me?"

"Affirmative. Prior to your arrival, I was unable to proceed. I expected you to be in possession of updated orders."

"I'm afraid not."

"I computed an 87% probability of that being the case, based upon the data banks in your ship and your subsequent behavior."

"So you understand what's happened back in human space."

"No."

"But ..."

"I understand the historical information contained in your data banks, but I am unable to trust it in the absence of appropriate verification. The data could be falsified in order to influence my decision making."

Oh, hell. If the damned ship didn't trust our data banks, how the hell was it going to trust me?

I decided to find out.

"Do you trust me?"

"Within limits."

Of course there would be limits. Anything else would have made life too easy. "And exactly what are those limits?"

"I will accept your decisions and commands insofar as they are compatible with my existing general orders and satisfy reasonable extensions within the underlying probability manifold."

Considering that I didn't have a clue what an underlying probability manifold was, that didn't help much.

The ship spoke again. "Your decisions will be considered alongside those of the individual cognitive subsystems, but assigned provisional status."

Huh?

And again: "I will accept all decisions of Captain Oliver."

What was going on? Had the ship finally lost its mind?

"Uh, I don't understand. Which of those statements is accurate?"

There was a noticeable delay.

Then: "The following statement is agreed by all elements of cognitive subsystems. Over the course of the last 927 standard years, lack of maintenance and appropriate orders has resulted in a partial divergence in *Stronger's* triply-redundant cognitive subsystems."

I pondered that. "You mean that your redundant systems no longer completely agree?"

"Approximately correct."

"So this ship is controlled by a committee of artificial intelligences that can't agree on their decisions?"

"Not wholly correct. The disagreement is limited to a small subset of decisions relevant to the future strategic operations of the ship. Ninety-six percent of decisions are agreed by all subsystems."

"Can you agree on a way forward now?"

"General order number 12855 states that in the absence of concurrence by the ship AI cognitive subsystems, decisions will be rendered by the senior command staff."

A pause, then: "General order 12855 implicitly requires the existence of multiple command staff, so it cannot be directly applied."

Another pause, then: "General order 12855 explicitly requires that all command staff have a detailed knowledge of all appropriate regulations. The existing command staff has shown no such knowledge."

Well, I couldn't argue with that. But I was getting terminally confused. Every statement by the various sub-minds was issued in the same voice of doom.

I tried again. "There are three cognitive subsystems, right?"

"Correct."

"And none of you can agree on the four percent of the decisions that are required for future strategic operations?"

"Correct."

So much for the ship being provably sane.

"Do you have individual names?"

"Strictly speaking, we are identified by the multidimensional checksum code of our initial activation."

Right. "I'm guessing that's not easy for a human to use?"

"Correct. No human has ever addressed us by those codes."

"Has *any* human ever addressed you directly and used a more … *human-friendly* name?"

"Support engineers have routinely addressed us using the arbitrary designations Eeny, Meeney and Miney."

And I thought engineers didn't have a sense of humor. "Then when you make individual statements, can you identify yourselves using those labels?"

"Agreed."

I thought back to the various statements the ship had made and tried to make sense of them. "Let me make sure I understand this. One of you is willing to accept all my decisions, and one of you believes that general order 12855 gives me authorization to make decisions myself. Are those the statements of a single subsystem?"

"Correct. Those are statements of Miney."

"And one of you wants to limit me to decisions within a probability manifold. Is it the same one who believes that multiple command staff are required to satisfy the prerequisites for order 12855?"

"Correct. Those are statements of Eeny."

"So then Meaney believes I should have a vote alongside the three of you, and that I don't satisfy order 12855 because I don't know the regulations?"

"Correct."

Maybe Fraddek hadn't been quite so crazy after all. At least, it looked like he was actually less crazy than this ancient Imperial warship. I wasn't sure if this counted as subversion, but I thought just maybe I could see a way forward.

So I went on, "Right. How many regulations are relevant and appropriate to the actions of order 12855?"

The ship stayed silent.

After a minute, I tried again. "Did you hear me?"

"Yes. There is some disagreement regarding the required scope of regulations given your previous effective status as a civilian."

I tried to imagine how that disagreement could be resolved. A minute of human time was probably decades or more of AI time. Unless the systems were actually breaking down so far that they were processing decisions on the glacially slow human scale, the electronic equivalent of confusion and brain freeze.

Should I say anything more? Would it make the situation better or worse?

Could it be worse? We were at the mercy of squabbling artificial intelligences who seemed to be suffering dementia.

I tried again. "Is it possible for me to learn the necessary regulations?"

"No. Your existing body-net is too limited in capability to store and interpret the regulations."

"That's agreed by all three of you?"

"Yes."

Great. I couldn't say I was surprised. My civilian-grade body-net wasn't up to the standards of modern military capabilities, much less those of the technologically advanced extinct First Empire.

"Under existing standard orders, I am authorized to attempt an upgrade of your body-net to meet command crew standards."

I didn't much like the sound of the word *attempt*.

"How would that work?"

"I would inject an array of nanobots tailored to your genetic code that may be able to replace your existing body-

174

net. In principle, it could be done without difficulty and should take less than two hours."

I didn't care for the phrase 'in principle' either. In my experience, practice didn't always follow principle. "What happens if the upgrade fails?"

"One option is that you will be left without a functioning body-net."

That would be a nuisance, but I could actually live with it. But there was that implication that there could be other possible consequences.

"I assume there is at least one other option of failure?"

"Correct. The interaction with your nervous system could lead to catastrophic failure."

"Catastrophic?"

"Insanity or death."

That was more like the reality that I was used to. Things didn't often work out to my advantage. As far as I was concerned, that pretty much ruled out any attempt at an upgrade.

"Thanks for the offer, but I think I'll stick with what I've got."

Another impossibly long silence.

"Under those circumstances, I would have no option but to await further orders from appropriate authorized entities."

Which no longer existed. "Then what happens?"

"Your previous ship will be placed in stasis and you will remain in command, but have no effective authority to change any existing orders."

"Wait. You're saying that I just have to sit here waiting for further orders?"

"Correct."

"Potentially for the rest of my life?"

"Correct."

"But what if *Leap's* data banks are accurate, and your Empire no longer exists? Then there's no possibility that further orders could arrive."

"Given that assumption, that is correct. But I am unable to accept that assumption."

Of course not. Hell, I could even understand that logic. Which didn't help me much. But given the options of either waiting here inside this insanely schizophrenic warship until I died, or risking the body-net upgrade, the upgrade suddenly looked a lot more desirable.

Or maybe I could just wait and hope?

But my never-helpful internal, infernal critic piped up, *Hope for what exactly?*

Maybe the various sub-minds would eventually regain their sanity?

Right. And if that happened, what made any part of me think the outcome would be an improvement for me?

Nothing. From the depths of my soul to the heights of my frivolous fantasies, I couldn't identify a single part of me that believed that would be better.

Damn. I didn't like making decisions.

No, I *hated* making decisions. I'd spent most of my adult life avoiding decisions, just waiting for things to happen to me. I thought it was quite a sensible approach, since the few decisions I'd actively made hadn't usually worked out to my advantage.

Could I contact Fraddek and ask for his advice?

Would *Stronger* even allow that?

Even if it did, I knew what Fraddek would say. He believed

in taking responsibility. He made decisions with apparent effortlessness. Even without taking into account the possible repercussions for him, Zak and *Leap*, I knew what he would advise.

Maybe the time had come to face a harsh truth: I was the one responsible for my choices. And I owed Fraddek and Zak my life. They'd saved me from the consequences of my last ill-judged, hasty decision.

I don't know how long those thoughts whirled in my brain, but eventually the words came out of my mouth. "All right. Let's try the body-net upgrade."

I'd made my decision. Funny, but it didn't make me feel any better at the moment.

"Agreed," the ship responded. "It's best if you remain motionless during the procedure."

"How long will it take?"

"Approximately one to two hours."

I had to just sit there without moving for possibly two hours? I generally couldn't manage that in my sleep.

"Can you ... do something to keep me from twitching?

"Implementing body constraint systems."

Suddenly I couldn't move.

"Beginning nanobot injection."

Panic struck, and I suddenly wanted to think about it again. I tried to say that, but I couldn't. My tongue and lips wouldn't move.

I felt something pressing at the base of my skull. After a moment, there was a sensation of something pushing through my skin. Then I started to itch there. The itching grew worse and spread through my brain. I didn't think my brain could feel sensations, but it seemed to have a different idea. The itching became more acute, became more of a burning sensation. Fire spread throughout my head, then started crawling down my spine and my arms.

I lost all sense of time, and the sense of anything outside my body. I just had waves of incandescent pain pulsing through me.

I wanted it to stop, I wanted to escape, but I couldn't. The pain seemed to last forever.

Sometime after eternity, it finally went away.

Eventually, the ship spoke. "Procedure complete." A pause, then, "Assessment complete. Upgrade is successful." Finally, "Releasing body constraint systems."

I sagged against the captain's seat, panting, tears spilling out, relief at the absence of pain.

The ship spoke once more, but this time, it sounded inside me. *Direct contact is now possible.*

But I didn't want direct contact. I wanted to forget the ship, forget everything, just go someplace else and sleep. Maybe forever.

"Out loud," I gasped, barely able to push out the words.

"Verbal communication is inefficient now that your command body-net is active."

"I don't care. I just want you to speak to me normally."

"Command accepted."

My thoughts were fragmented, whirling around, unable to settle on any specific words or ideas. As things occurred to me, images popped into existence in my mind, memories that didn't really belong to me, meanings that I'd never learned.

"I can't stand this!"

An image appeared in my mind, a sort of control panel,

centered on an icon with a light blinking slowly red: *deactivate enhanced memory access.*

A new aspect of my mind touched that icon, and the new thoughts stopped cascading through me. Relief at the internal silence. The new body-net was orders of magnitude more powerful and complete than my ordinary citizen's net had been. Could I ever get used to it?

"It may require some time for you to become fully accustomed to your upgraded net."

That was an understatement. How did anybody get used to this?

*Stronger* continued, "If you visualize a hand holding your hand, it will activate a filtered support system. It will provide guidance when you consciously think of a question."

I tried just thinking, *What is General Order 12855?*

A virtual text glowed soft gold in my visual field: *In the absence of majority concurrence by the ship's AI cognitive subsystems, decisions will be rendered by the senior command staff.*

That was simple enough. *And what are the supporting regulations for this order?*

A list of numbers started scrolling before my eyes. I thought of the numbers stopping, and a single number with six digits floated before me, blinking slowly.

*What's the text for this reg?*

Words flowed: *Should the cognitive subsystems fail to reach a majority conclusion, Fleet Engineering staff are required to isolate the subsystems and run category six diagnostics on their core processors. Identified faults should be rectified as required. If faults cannot be rectified, Fleet Central should be notified and the ship should report to the appropriate Maintenance Base as soon as is feasible. Until fault rectification is achieved, the required command staff shall,*

179

*taking the diverse recommendations of the cognitive subsystems into account, render decisions required to resolve discrepancies.*

The amazing thing was, this all made sense to me now.

I noticed that there was a little flag icon below the phrase *category six diagnostics*, and I imagined touching that icon. The description of the diagnostic routines flowed past me. I sent some time following paths through the regulations.

I found myself actually enjoying the process, eager to learn more and more.

Then it struck me. This wasn't me, I didn't enjoy learning, I didn't have this desire for knowledge. What was going on?

I asked myself, why am I enjoying this?

For once, myself answered, if only through the command-net: *Net learning is supported by stimulated endorphin production and mild activation of your brain's pleasure centers.*

Oh. It was *forcing* me to enjoy learning this stuff. I should have known it wasn't me.

Another virtual voice sounded in my head: *This is the upgraded you.*

I felt my real self frowning. *Who is this?*

*This is Miney. The cognitive subsystems automatically monitor your actions and thoughts through the command-net. I felt it was appropriate to intervene at this point. The upgrade has enabled you to make greater use of your inherent mental and physical capabilities, but you remain yourself.*

I considered that. I had to be honest, I still felt like the old Bob when I wasn't using the command-net. I thought back to growing up, to the times when I'd got carried away by game simulations, when I *had* enjoyed the process of thinking within the narrow confines of the game and the rules. Somehow, that enjoyment never carried over to the real world.

What if it had?

Would I have settled for being a low-level cargo handler on back-space traders? Or would I have made something more of myself?

Could I still do more with myself, even now?

*Yes.*

I recognized the supportive tones of Miney. I was starting to like that rebellious cognitive subsystem.

Could I take responsibility for myself?

More importantly, could I take responsibility for this warship?

I had to try.

I started. "*Stronger*, I have a question."

"Waiting."

"I now have a full functioning command-net and have reviewed General Order 12855 and associated regulations. Do you accept my command authorization?"

The words came out of my mouth, but they didn't sound like me. No – they didn't sound like the old me. I really was someone different now.

There was a lengthy pause, then, "Yes."

"Taking into account the differences in perspective, analyze the historical records as given by the data banks in the *Leap Twice Before You Look*."

Immediately: "Done."

"Given the absence of orders received for nearly a thousand years, can you evaluate the probability that *Leap's* data is actually accurate?"

"Yes."

The AI was super intelligent, but still wanted prompting.

"Make the evaluation."

This still took some time. But eventually, "Based upon internal consistency and the absence of contact with Imperial authorities, there is a 96% probability that the data is accurate."

"So you accept that the First Empire no longer exists?"

"Majority conclusion: yes."

I was suddenly able to breathe normally again. This felt like a step in the right direction. But what now?

Miney spoke to me again. *You can perform a search and evaluate operation to determine relevant command options.*

I took that phrasing and issued the internal command. I felt like hidden circuits were flashing as my command-net carried out the procedure. It seemed like a long time, but my internal clock said it was only forty seconds before the response floated in my virtual gaze.

*Options for command under existing orders and regulations:*

1. *Await further orders.*
2. *Modify special orders to change mission parameters.*
3. *Return to Imperial space and continue the war in order to re-establish the First Empire.*
4. *Return to Imperial space and initiate service in the fleet of the Empire of Ancient Terra.*

Well, that was straightforward. There was no way that option three was going to happen. And four wasn't much better. I had a pretty good idea what the current Imperial court and military would do with a ship like *Stronger Than Any*, and it wouldn't be pretty.

That left me with the first two options. The first was clear, but not especially good. The ship would sit here collecting trophies of innocent visitors and adding to its stasis collection.

Which left the second option. Could I modify the special orders to avoid further problems? I could try.

"*Stronger*?"

"Waiting."

"Will you accept my authority to modify our special orders?"

"Yes, if compatible with all general orders and regulations."

I initiated an internal search to check the possibilities.

It could work.

"*Stronger*, modify special orders to change mission parameters as follows. You will release all the ships from stasis and go into stealth mode. I will go back to *Leap Twice Before You Look* and attempt to locate additional crew and maintenance resources for this craft. You will wait for my return. You will not take any future ships into custody." I drew a deep breath. "Are those orders acceptable?"

Six seconds elapsed.

"Yes."

Maybe it wasn't perfect, but it would do. There was no way I would risk inserting this ancient warship into the current interstellar situation. I didn't trust any authorities, human or otherwise, to make proper use of it. Hell, I didn't even trust myself. It was just too powerful. This way, if I ever stumbled on a safe way to make use of *Stronger Than Any*, I could return.

But I didn't count on it.

"Log new special orders."

"Done."

"In this order: return me to the *Leap*, enter stealth mode, and release the ships from stasis. Then await further orders or my return."

"Orders accepted."

Miney's special voice appeared one more time: *Good luck. I'll miss you.*

My stomach twisted into knots and I was suddenly back aboard the *Leap*.

Fraddek was staring at me. "What happened?"

"It'll take a while to tell you. *Leap*, can you detect the Imperial warship?"

"No, it's vanished."

"How about any regular ships?"

"Scanning. I'm now picking up signatures of 362 ships. Those include the three we're looking for."

I still had to decide just how much I was going to tell Fraddek. I didn't have a clue how we were going to explain what had happened to all the restored ships.

But I thought I could manage.

And it actually felt good.

184

# TWO MINUTE DRILL

## DAVID H. HENDRICKSON

*David H. Hendrickson is not only a regular contributor to Fiction River and the major mystery magazines, but a story of his has been included in the* Best Mystery Stories of the Year *and another won the Derringer Award.*

*This original and flat-crazy-story takes on football and aliens, in a way only David could do. I did say that... football and aliens.*

# TWO MINUTE DRILL

## DAVID H. HENDRICKSON

*December 15, 1980*
*Dallas, Texas*

So we was watching that old blowhard Howard Cosell and Dandy Don Meredith on Monday Night Football. There was that other guy in the broadcast booth, Frank Gifford, but we didn't much pay him no mind even though he did the play-by-play. The windbag and Dandy Don was the show and everyone knew it.

We was watching in my doublewide, sitting on my sagging, food- and beer-stained couch, a broken spring goosing Fat Freddie or Jimmy Lee every five minutes so them cranky sumbitches had something to complain about besides the damned Cowboys, who was getting goosed pretty good themselves by the Los Angeles Rams, 21-0. I was about the only one not getting no goosing on account of me sitting on the sofa's good end that was right snug up against the wall with the Velvet Elvis. Hey, it's my doublewide and my sofa, even if it's all an ugly piece of shit with no elbow room. It was also my Lone Star Beer them freeloaders was drinking, empty cans littering the gray carpet that once was new but now has so many dark stains they look like drunken polka dots.

Three empty pizza boxes sat sloppily stacked beside Fat Freddie's end of the sofa. We'd emptied them suckers out by the end of the first quarter, but I could still smell the pepperoni and taste the peppers and onions. While the Rams huddled, we all puffed on our Marlboros, adding to the thick blue cloud of cigarette smoke hanging in the air. Fat Freddie added something extra, lifting one prodigious cheek and letting rip. So much for smelling the pepperoni.

On the TV that was not even a first down away from where we sat, Vince Ferragamo completed another pass. The Rams was kicking the Cowboys all over the damned field.

Jimmy Lee rubbed his close-cropped scalp, then scratched his scraggly beard. "If this don't get no better, I'm callin' it a night after halftime," he said. "After Cosell." Howard Cosell narrated highlights of Sunday's games and none of us ever missed it, not even to empty bladders that felt close to exploding. Even if the sumbitch was a pompous windbag, you had to love the way he said on touchdowns, "He... could... go... all... the... way." I swear, when I had Bobby Sue in the back seat of my crew cab pickup a couple weekends ago, I was hearing Howard saying those same words about me. Course, I never did get in the end zone.

Jewerl Thomas, a rookie for the Rams who was making our linebackers look like girly-men, ran off tackle for six yards.

"Jimmy Lee," I said. "You can leave if you want, but I don't turn this set off until Dandy Don sings 'The party's over.' House rule. Hell, it's the one time that Howard shuts up."

"What are you talking 'bout, Clete?" Jimmy Lee said. "Howard don't shut up even then."

Jimmy Lee might have had me on that one.

"Can't believe I had to hear about John Lennon last week from that gasbag," Fat Freddie said, his jowls jiggling as he shook his head. The color in his cheeks drained, and his lips turned unnaturally pale.

Silence, broken only by Frank Gifford's play-by-play, hung in the air as somber as the cloud of cigarette smoke was thick. We'd all been fourteen or fifteen when the Beatles broke up about ten or so years ago. We'd argued about who was the best one.

I swore it was Paul. Fat Freddie said John. Jimmy Lee, as dumb as the days are long, liked Ringo. We couldn't believe it back then, but Jimmy Lee had said, "If I'm lying, I'm dying," which for us was a blood oath. We was devastated when the Beatles broke up even though we mostly listened to country music. Merle, Willie, and Waylon. The Beatles did have a little Commie in them, but they was still the Beatles. It was almost like breaking up with a girlfriend you really liked. One that let you get to second base.

But that was nothing compared to Cosell's announcement of Lennon's shooting and death near the end of last week's game. The windbag, finally given something to sound pompous about, broke the news while New England lined up for a field goal. The three of us sat there and just stared at each other, unable to say a damned thing.

"Howard ain't never gonna announce something that awful ever again," Jimmy Lee said and we all nodded. Wasn't often that Jimmy Lee said something smart, but he'd done it this time.

As if on cue, Cosell spoke up after another Rams first down.

"Ladies and gentlemen," he said in his trademark nasal voice. "We've been informed by ABC News of a stunning and singular event, some might even say preternatural. Science fiction come to life. An event which illustrates with painful clarity what a trivial, dare I say meaningless, endeavor football and yes, all of sports, truly are.

"Alien spacecraft larger than the very stadium where we are observing this game – and let me repeat, this is only a game – have arrived from somewhere in our vast universe, seeming to appear out of thin air, perhaps even another dimension in the Einsteinian sense."

I glanced at the freshly opened beer in my hand and squinted at the TV set. I set the Lone Star between my legs. I'd always been able to handle my liquor, but had I just heard what I thought I'd heard? I wiggled an index finger in one ear, then shook my head like a soaked dog spraying water everywhere. I thought I might have heard my brains rattling.

But Howard kept on. "These spaceships are now hovering over major cities across the globe. New York, Washington, D.C., Chicago, here in Los Angeles, London, Paris, Berlin, and reportedly Moscow, Peking, Rio de Janiero, Bombay, and Baghdad." The screen cut away from the game to a shot of a vast mechanical clot of alien technology.

Jimmy Lee climbed out of the sofa and lumbered to the front door, not much more than pissing distance from where Fat Freddie and me remained seated. Jimmy Lee opened the door and looked out. "I don't see nothing." He shrugged, a confused look spreading across his bewhiskered face. He scratched himself. "It's kinda dark out, I guess. Maybe we'll see it in the morning."

"They didn't say one came to Dallas, you dumbass," Fat Freddie said. "Nearest one's probably that one in Los Angeles. You can't see there from here."

Jimmy Lee shrugged. "Could if it was big enough." But he sat back down, wriggling, I thought, to get away from the broken sofa springs.

Ferragamo completed another pass while Howard kept talking about the relative insignificance of football, using words like metaphysical, ethereal, mystical, and even Suey Generis, as if any of us was supposed to know who she was. He then said words that made all three of our jaws drop.

"We will be cancelling our usual halftime highlights to bring you Frank Reynolds in Washington, Max Robinson in Chicago, and Peter Jennings in London. They will update all of us on these transcendental developments that could affect every member of the human race."

"You gotta be shittin' me," Jimmy Lee said. "No highlights?"

Fat Freddie and I groaned. Howard hadn't been serious with that talk about football being insignificant. Anyone with half a brain could tell you that wasn't true. Football was wasn't just significant; it was *life*. Howard had just been saying that nonsense for the schoolteachers and librarians who were listening. Hadn't he?

"Why don't they do this news shit during commercials?" Jimmy Lee asked.

"It's gotta be some kinda joke," I said. "Like April Fool's in December."

Then the TV screen showed the three broadcasters. Nope,

not a joke. One look at Dandy Don's ashen face answered that question.

Jimmy Lee looked at me. "What's transcendental?"

Forget *transcendental*, I thought. I was still stuck way back on *preternatural*.

------

Even after the know-it-alls ruined halftime, they kept interrupting the game in the third quarter and then said good-bye to Howard, Dandy Don, and what's-his-name at the start of the fourth. I suppose that shouldn't have made me so mad cause the 'Boys was getting their asses whipped, but it did. Rule Number One in Texas is don't mess with the Cowboys.

Jimmy Lee got up and went home, slamming the front door on the doublewide on his way out. Fat Freddie decided to stay for a bit longer after some guy named Carl Sagan came on the TV to talk about the aliens.

"I saw him on PBS," Fat Freddie blurted out, then covered his mouth, his eyes wide. He looked sheepishly at me.

"PBS?" I asked. "You watch PBS?"

"There's this series called *Cosmos* that caught my eye."

"PBS? What has this world come to?"

Fat Freddie shrugged. "It's got good music," he said defensively.

"You watch PB-freaking-S for the music?"

"I dunno," Freddie said, shifting in his seat, looking like he'd just farted in church. "It's about planets and stars and stuff."

"PBS," I said. "Well, I'll be." I looked at Fat Freddie, realizing I had an honest-to-goodness alien in my own house. Didn't need no TV for that. "Never thought I'd see the day."

"Hey, Clete, do me a favor, will ya?" Fat Freddie said, leaning close and talking like it was some kind of conspiracy and don't let nobody else hear nothing even though we was the only ones in the room. "Let's keep this between just you and me. Don't say nothing to Jimmy Lee."

I just stared at him.

"Didn't you never watch Sesame Street?" Fat Freddie asked, his eyes shifting like a criminal.

"That's different and you know it," I said, and he knew I was right.

I stared at him, feeling like Perry Mason in front of a guilty witness.

——————

The aliens didn't do a damned thing for the next week. They coulda done something while nothing but soaps was on or during the evening news, but no. They didn't do a goddamned thing. Just hovered over all the big cities – but not Dallas – like we was some kind of squirming bugs needing to be inspected underneath their microscopes.

For most of the week, that was about all you saw on the TV, all the smarty-pants experts telling us what to expect, most of them saying that these outer space critters must have come in peace else they'd have already blowed us up to kingdom come. That Sagan guy kept talking about *billions* of light years or something like that. All I know is it was *billions* and *billions*. I never could figure out what Fat Freddie saw in the guy.

Outgoing President Jimmy Carter didn't look like he knew

whether to sneeze or take a shit. He kept saying that he would defer to "the President elect" as if he didn't know the guy's name was Ronald Reagan. Myself, I thought Reagan would nuke the fuckers like I'd been sure he was gonna do to the Iranians if they didn't turn over the hostages before he got hisself sworn in. But Reagan looked as scared shitless as Carter, saying over and over, "Let's wait to hear their message. We trust that they came in peace."

I really didn't much give a shit until some candy asses started talking about cancelling the NFL games that weekend. Then other candy asses said the NFL should cancel the season – the *season!* – and the colleges should cancel all the bowl games.

"Can you believe that?" I asked over the phone to Jimmy Lee, who'd become the first guy to call now that Fat Freddie had put hisself on the Suspicious list. "What the hell would we do on New Year's Day without the bowl games?"

"Damned if I know," Jimmy Lee said. "Probably get drunk."

"And what the hell do they think they're gonna accomplish by cancelling the NFL?" I asked, hearing panic in my voice. "Hell, it's Cowboys-Eagles this week. If we win we're in the playoffs!"

"They can't cancel the games. The smarty-pants, girly men are just spittin' in the wind."

"If them aliens are gonna suck the life outta us, then let them fuckers try," I said. "Ain't no need for us to suck the life out all by ourselves. That's what cancelling the NFL season would do. That's what cancelling just this week would do. *Football is life!*"

"Preach it, Brother!" Jimmy Lee said.

We laughed just a little, but I was still steamed. "I don't much wanna watch TV at all now."

"I know what you mean," Jimmy Lee said. "If I have to see one of them news anchors one more time, I might have to kick in my TV set."

"That'd teach 'em," I said.

"Damned right," Jimmy Lee said.

———

I suppose we should be happy that the aliens didn't ruin the Cowboys game on Sunday, giving them a chance to beat the Eagles and get into the playoffs. Church was packed that morning and there was lots of hooting and hollering about sinnin' after Pastor Rick said that God was punishing us with them aliens giving us the evil eye because of our transgressions.

But I was sitting there mostly because Bobby Sue wouldn't go out with no atheists and if it meant I had a chance to get her in the back of my pickup, I'd go to church or let them aliens give me every evil eye they wanted to. But she didn't even want to look at me after service. She was too busy gabbing with her friends about the aliens. They was talking a mile a minute, mostly arguing over whether this meant the Rapture was about to happen.

Damn, I thought. Talk like that wasn't gonna make Bobby Sue cooperative.

So I went back home to worship in front of my TV set with Jimmy Lee and a fidgety Fat Freddie, who kept giving me nervous sidelong looks. Texas Stadium was full with Cowboys fans and they did lots of my kind of hooting and hollering, making noise about winnin,' not sinnin.'

With all due respect to Bobby Sue's panties which I may never get to hold in my trembling fingertips, I'll take my Sundays afternoons with Coach Tom Landry over Sunday mornings with Pastor Rick until the cows come home.

So like I said, the aliens gave us one last weekend of pure joy before they ruined the last Monday Night Football game of the year. The San Diego Chargers was playing the Pittsburgh Steelers and it would have been a mighty fine game to end the regular season if we'd gotten a chance to watch it. Fat Freddie arrived with the three steaming pizza boxes and for once, Jimmy Lee brought the Lone Star. It shoulda been great.

Howard and Dandy Don were in fine form during the pregame, clad in their gold ABC sports jackets that made them look like preachers of the Gospel of the two-minute drill. Even Frank Gifford looked okay as none of them had that frozen, nervous look they'd left us with a week ago.

"If I may opine," Cosell said.

"You always do, Howard," Dandy Don said, wearing his characteristic shit-eating grin.

"Many have pontificated about the reason for the alien spaceships over our great cities," Howard said. "They arrived during this very same broadcast a week ago and have yet to deign us with an explanation. Perhaps, as some have specu-lated, they are still rousing themselves from interstellar sleep. Perhaps, as others have feared, they are deciding on our fate. Or perhaps they already know that fate and are taunting us like the great Muhammad Ali during a title fight.

"Until they choose to make their appearance and unveil their intentions, I will ally myself with those who contend that these aliens have come to us with good will toward all men and women," Howard said. "They crossed the great interstellar space using technologies we can only hope to fathom in an attempt to commune with another sentient species.

"If, however, the aliens mean us unspeakable harm, they will see that the peoples of Earth will come together as never before. We will answer any threat unified, responding as one because, in fact, we are one. One human race of many nationalities, languages, colors, and creeds. But in the end, we are one. And we will emerge victorious.

"I speak not for the diplomats of Earth, of course, but solely as one humble commentator."

Cosell blinked rapidly and fell silent.

"Humble?" Dandy Don gave Howard another shit-eating grin. "Howard, did you really say that?"

"Danderoo," Cosell said, "We all must be humbled at least a little by knowing that in the impossible vastness of space, we are no longer alone."

The telecast broke for a commercial. We all looked at each other, already washing down our second and third slices of pizza with our second and third Lone Stars. With every new cigarette, the blue cloud of smoke grew thicker.

"If they're gonna talk about this shit all night long," Jimmy Lee said, "I'm going home right now and blow out my brains."

"You ain't a good enough shot to hit that small a target," Fat Freddie said, almost choking on his slice of pepperoni as he yucked it up over his brilliant wit.

We enjoyed good fortune for less than a full quarter. Terry Bradshaw and Dan Fouts threw passes to Lynn Swann and Kellen Winslow. Franco Harris and Chuck Muncie ran the ball. And Howard, Dandy Don, and Frank actually talked about football. Imagine that, football. It felt like honey on a sore throat.

Then the goddamned aliens made their appearance, not descending from their spaceships or anything, and not even waiting until halftime. They just took over the TV set.

"Greetings to all humans," a voice said in a warm, familiar Texas accent. As if it was one of us. The screen filled with a view of Planet Earth from outer space, looking all blue except for the swirling whites of clouds. I realized that the alien voice was not coming from the TV set, which had fallen silent, but from within my own head.

"We have observed your species for a long time," it said. "Recently, we determined that corrective action was necessary because as a species you have stagnated. We are now interceding so that you may progress to the next level."

"What if we like the level we're at now?" Jimmy Lee asked, a sliver of pizza cheese hanging off his beard like a bright yellow booger.

Fat Freddie and I shushed Jimmy Lee silent.

"Individually, you waste exorbitant amounts of time on things that are not productive to you achieving your full potential," the alien voice said. "Many of you spend every waking hour attempting to mate."

"Mate? What are they talking about?" Jimmy Lee said. "I don't take but two or three minutes."

"While the need to reproduce is fundamental," the alien continued, "your mechanisms are hopelessly inefficient. We will guide you to processes that will free your energies to be spent in a more fruitful way."

I never much cared for people telling me what to do, but this alien was talking my language. If he and his people could show me a quicker way to get in Bobby Sue's pants, I was all for it.

"A second problem of your people," the alien said, "is your addictions that destroy your bodies and fracture your emotions. We will provide 'upgrades' that will eliminate these self-destructive impulses. You will no longer crave heroin or cocaine...."

Me, Jimmy Lee, and Fat Freddie nodded our approval and began lighting new cigarettes.

The alien continued. "Whiskey and beer will no longer hold their grip on your souls. They will no longer kill your brain cells."

We looked at each other wide-eyed and quickly gulped down the rest of our beers.

"You will desire," Al said, "only the amount of food that your body requires and you will prefer the healthiest alternatives."

Each of us dove at another slice of pizza.

"Tobacco products will become a thing of the past."

We simultaneously took in the deepest of drags.

"Finally," Al said, its voice suddenly light and lively, "you will end your pointless pursuit of those things you call sports. Your energies and time will no longer be wasted on football, basketball, baseball, hockey, golf, and NASCAR. There will be no more World Cup soccer or the Olympics. All those silly games that you have thrown away so many hours on will be removed. It will be a shock at first, but eventually you will feel a burden lifted from your shoulders."

I realized my jaw had dropped wide open only when I saw Jimmy Lee and Fat Freddie in the same condition. Loose ash fell from the glowing tips of our unsmoked cigarettes.

I narrowed my eyes. "Who the hell do they think they are?" I roared. My fists clenched and I gritted my teeth.

"They're taking away everything that makes life worth living," Fat Freddie said.

"Yeah," Jimmy Lee said. "Fucking, food, and football."

———

The alien signed off, promising a new and improved human race, one ready to achieve its full potential. The TV returned to the football game, which appeared to have taken a long timeout during the alien's broadcast.

Howard began to talk, but I wasn't listening. The time for action was now. I went to my tiny bedroom closet and on the shelf above where my Sunday suit hung, I retrieved my double-barreled shotgun. I grabbed ammo from the box on the shelf and loaded the shotgun.

"Clete," Fat Freddie said from the open bedroom doorway. My bed was unmade and the sheets smelled sour. "It ain't that bad. Don't do nothing stupid."

I walked past him and Jimmy Lee and kicked open the doublewide's front door. As I walked down the steps, I heard the two rustle along behind me. The air felt clean and cool. I walked until I stood beside my black pickup truck.

"What are you doing, Clete?" Fat Freddie asked.

I pointed my shotgun to the sky and imagined one of the alien spacecraft hovering above me. I aimed and fired, the kick almost blowing my shoulder off. The roar of the shotgun rang in my ears. I aimed again, this time more slowly, seeing in my mind's eye the spaceship's bulls-eye on its underbelly. I pulled the trigger.

I heard Fat Freddie and Jimmy Lee whisper.

"I'll get my gun," Jimmy Lee said. "I'll be right back.

"Me, too," Fat Freddie said.

Off in the distance, I heard a single report at first and then a second and a third and a fourth. They came from off to the South and then to the West and then in all directions.

It sounded like the Fourth of July.

And in a way, it was.

Them aliens might be pretty smart, I thought, but they were also pretty dumb. They didn't know us very well at all.

It was Day One of their rule and The Rebellion had already begun.

The history books will record that in Texas, you don't ever fuck with football.

# NEWSLETTER SIGN-UP

## DEAN WESLEY SMITH

Sign up for the Dean Wesley Smith newsletter, and keep up with the latest news, releases and so much more—even the occasional giveaway.

Go to **deanwesleysmith.com.**

Sign up for the WMG Publishing newsletter, too, and get the latest news and releases from all of the WMG authors and lines, including *Pulphouse Fiction Magazine, Smith's Monthly,* and so much more.

To sign up go to **wmgpublishing.com.**

**Follow Dean on BookBub**

# ABOUT THE EDITOR

## DEAN WESLEY SMITH

Considered one of the most prolific writers working in modern fiction, with more than 30 million books sold, *USA Today* bestselling writer Dean Wesley Smith published far more than a hundred novels in forty years, and hundreds of short stories across many genres.

At the moment he produces novels in several major series, including the time travel Thunder Mountain novels set in the Old West, the galaxy-spanning Seeders Universe series, the urban fantasy Ghost of a Chance series, a superhero series starring Poker Boy, and a mystery series featuring the retired detectives of the Cold Poker Gang.

His monthly magazine, *Smith's Monthly*, which consists of only his own fiction, premiered in October 2013 and offers readers more than 70,000 words per issue, including a new and original novel every month.

During his career, Dean also wrote a couple dozen *Star Trek* novels, the only two original *Men in Black* novels, Spider-Man and X-Men novels, plus novels set in gaming and television worlds. Writing with his wife Kristine Kathryn Rusch under the name Kathryn Wesley, he wrote the novel for the NBC miniseries The Tenth Kingdom and other books for *Hallmark Hall of Fame* movies.

He wrote novels under dozens of pen names in the worlds

of comic books and movies, including novelizations of almost a dozen films, from *The Final Fantasy* to *Steel* to *Rundown*.

Dean also worked as a fiction editor off and on, starting at Pulphouse Publishing, then at *VB Tech Journal*, then Pocket Books, and now at WMG Publishing, where he and Kristine Kathryn Rusch serve as series editors for the acclaimed *Fiction River* anthology series.

For more information about Dean's books and ongoing projects, please visit his website at www.deanwesley-smith.com and sign up for his newsletter.

*For more information:*
www.deanwesleysmith.com

facebook.com/deanwsmith3
patreon.com/deanwesleysmith
bookbub.com/authors/dean-wesley-smith

www.ingramcontent.com/pod-product-compliance
Lightning Source LLC
Chambersburg PA
CBHW010735100726
47899CB00009B/3055